The Mystery
of the
Black Schooner

THE MYSTERY OF THE BLACK SCHOONER

Based on the
television series
"FLIPPER" starring
Brian Kelly,
Luke Halpin,
and Tommy Norden.

By RICHARD HARDWICK

Illustrated by
AL ANDERSEN
and
ROBERT ALLEN

WHITMAN PUBLISHING COMPANY • Racine, Wisconsin

CONTENTS

Dedicated to
Tommy,
Richard,
and Les, Jr.

1. Visitors at Coral Key

The early morning sun glinted off the smooth waters of the lagoon at Coral Key as Bud Ricks leaned over the edge of the dock and poked the end of an old Klaxon horn beneath the surface. He gave the big horn a firm squeeze and there was a muted *honk!* under the water. At the same time Bud yelled, "Flipper! Flipper!"

The boy stood up slowly and squinted out toward the bay and the distant tiny islands that stood like green jewels at the edge of the vast expanse of the ocean beyond.

When half a minute or so had passed and nothing happened, a frown crossed the ten-year-old boy's freckled face. He waited a moment longer, then bent over to push the horn back into the water again.

But just as he did, something caught his attention, and he sat down on the edge of the dock and laid the horn aside as he watched curiously. Emerging slowly from beyond the northeast point at the mouth of the lagoon was a boat—but not the usual sort of outboard runabout Bud was accustomed to seeing around the bay. It was a beautiful sight. The long, low hull was painted a gleaming black, and three sparkling white sails, hoisted high on her two masts, pulled the schooner along with the faint morning breeze.

As the vessel rounded the point, the breeze was cut off by the tall palms and pines that grew along the shore. The sails began to flutter and luff. The schooner turned smoothly, losing headway as it did so. Bud saw that there were three men on deck. One stood at the helm in the cockpit, while the other two were standing near the masts. They loosened ropes, and suddenly the forward sail came piling down, then the middle sail, and finally the sternmost and largest of the sails dropped down in a cascade of billowing white canvas. One man stepped to the bow of the schooner and, with a splash, sent the anchor to the bottom of the lagoon. All three men then set about furling the sails.

"Wow!" Bud exclaimed. "What a boat!"

There was a sudden swirl of water a few yards out from the dock, and the intelligent face of a dolphin poked up, a mischievous grin on its long, narrow beak.

"Flipper!" Bud shouted, laughing.

The dolphin bobbed its head up and down and jabbered something that sounded to the boy as if the seagoing mammal might have said, "Good morning, Bud! Come on in. The water's fine!"

Bud pointed out toward the schooner, where the three men were just finishing furling the sails. A small boat with an outboard motor dangled at the end of a rope attached to the vessel's stern.

"Looks like we've got company, Flipper. I wonder who they are. You don't see a boat like that every day around Coral Key."

"We won't have to wait long to find out," said a voice behind him. Bud's older brother, Sandy, ambled across the dock and sat down beside him. "Good morning, Flipper," he said.

Flipper chattered in reply and gave his handsome head a shake. Rising up out of the water almost to the tip of his flukes, he moved backward across the water, trying to entice the boys into the water.

But at the moment the boys were much more interested in the black schooner. The three men had climbed down into the small boat and cast off the line. One of them gave the starter cord of the outboard motor a pull, there was a little puff of blue exhaust smoke, and the dinghy turned and headed straight in toward the dock.

As the boat drew near, Bud and Sandy saw that the man operating the motor was heavyset, with a bushy black moustache and a deep scowl on his sun-tanned face. The man on the center seat seemed to be the oldest of the trio, and there was something sad about his large, inquisitive eyes. He, too, had a moustache, but it was smaller and neater, and he had a short, pointed beard to go with it. The third man was the youngest. His black hair was crew cut, and he had the lean, loose body of an athlete.

The boat slowed and came alongside the dock. The youngest man tossed a line to Sandy, and as he tied it to a piling the big fellow shut off the motor.

The bearded man was first to speak. "Good morning, boys," he said. "May we come ashore?"

"Why, yes, sir," Sandy said.

The three men climbed onto the dock. The bearded man smiled at each of the boys. "Am I correct in assuming that this is Coral Key State Park and Marine Preserve?"

"Are you correct in a—what?" stammered Bud.

Sandy grinned and nodded. "Yes, sir, that's right."

"Good! I wonder, then, if you boys could direct us to the park ranger."

Sandy looked back toward the house on the low rise just above the dock. "We can in a few minutes. The park ranger is our dad, Porter Ricks. He drove down to the south campsite to check on some folks who are camping there, and he ought to be back in just a—" He broke off as a pickup truck appeared through the trees past the house. "Here he comes now."

"Fine. Now then, you've told us that your father's name is Mr. Porter Ricks. What might your names be?"

The big fellow who had been operating the boat grumbled, "What difference does that make, Professor?"

Bud's eyes popped. "Pro*fes*sor!" he mumbled, an expression of distaste wrinkling his brow as he made the connection between "professor" and "school." For Bud Ricks, education was one of those things that small boys were forced to endure—like eating spinach or being hugged by elderly aunts. "You mean you're—you're a *teacher?*"

The truck pulled to a halt at the end of the dock

and Park Ranger Porter Ricks got out. His gaze went from the schooner lying at anchor across the lagoon to the group on the dock.

"Good morning," he said with a smile. "I see my boys have already welcomed you to Coral Key."

"And a fine welcoming committee they are, Mr. Ricks," said the professor. "My name is Charles Avery." He nodded toward the big man. "This is Mel Latham, and my young companion here is Jack Finch."

Porter shook hands with each of them, then turned his attention back to the bearded man, his eyes narrowing with interest. "Are you by chance *Dr.* Charles Avery?"

"You mean he's a teacher *and* a doctor?" said Bud, appalled.

A peculiar expression flickered on the professor's face for a moment. Then he smiled and gave a little nod. "The same," he said.

Porter Ricks draped an arm around the shoulders of each of his sons. "This is quite an honor for us, boys, having Dr. Charles Avery drop in this way."

The two boys looked up at their father, puzzled, not understanding just what he meant. How was it that he knew this man who came sailing up practically out of the blue?

Seeing their confusion, Porter said, "Sandy, that book you've been reading lately—"

Sandy's mouth dropped open as he suddenly realized what his father meant. He stared at Dr. Avery. *"Spanish Shipwrecks of the New World!* That's the book! Are you *that* Dr. Charles Avery? The one who wrote the book?"

"I'm truly flattered that you've heard of me," the professor said, glancing momentarily at his two companions. "It's also most gratifying to know that my book is being read."

"It's terrific!" Sandy said excitedly. He turned to explain to Bud, who was still standing there with a totally blank look on his face. "It's all about the old days, Bud, when the Spaniards were taking all that gold and silver out of Mexico. A lot of their ships sunk or were wrecked on the way back to Spain and—" Suddenly he snapped his fingers. "I'll be right back!" he said, and he turned and dashed toward the house.

"Come on, Professor," Mel Latham growled impatiently. "Tell the ranger why we're here so we can get back to the 'Shark.' "

Dr. Avery nodded. "Quite right, Mel. Mr. Ricks, we'd like permission to anchor here in the lagoon for two or three weeks. Actually, we're preparing for

an expedition to the Caribbean Sea and the coast of
Central America. There are quite a few things that
need to be done to the ship. Also, several members
of our expedition will be joining us here in the weeks
to come, and the bay here would provide an excel-
lent place to test some of our equipment before we
leave and head south."

Bud scratched his head. "What's the shark?"

Jack Finch waggled a thumb toward the schooner.
"That's her. That's the 'Shark.' "

The boy shook his head dubiously. "Why did you
name a keen boat like that after just about the
dumbest old thing in the whole ocean?"

"Quiet, Son," Porter Ricks said. He turned back to
Dr. Avery. "You're welcome to anchor here for as
long as you like. In fact, it'll be a pleasure having
you as a neighbor. But wouldn't you be better off
docking at a marina or a boatyard?"

"True enough, in certain respects," the professor
agreed. "But it's been my experience that the men
are better prepared for a trip such as this when they
aren't too close to all the conveniences of a well-
equipped boatyard just before sailing. We can do
some practice diving on some of the wrecks that are
scattered about the marine preserve. You see, this
expedition will entail quite a bit of diving around

wrecks, and this will provide good practical experience. I can assure you, Mr. Ricks, that we shan't cause you one bit of bother."

"I'm sure of that, Dr. Avery," Porter replied. "I'd better get you a copy of the park regulations, however. Diving is permissible, but it's illegal to do any lobstering or spearfishing inside the marine preserve. Also, as I'm sure you already know, nothing is to be removed from any of the old wrecks you might find on the reefs."

"Of course." The professor nodded. "That's the primary purpose of the marine preserve, to keep the area from being despoiled."

"Bud," Porter said, "run up to the house and get a copy of the regulations out of my desk."

Sandy came dashing pell-mell onto the dock, a book clutched in his hands. He thrust the book and a pen at Dr. Avery. "It's my copy of *Spanish Shipwrecks of the New World,* sir. Will you autograph it for me?"

"I'll be delighted," the professor said, smiling. He signed it and returned it to the boy.

Mel Latham tapped him on the arm impatiently. "Come on, Professor. We've got plenty of work to do."

"It's been a pleasure meeting you," the professor

said to Porter and Sandy. "We'll pick up the regulations later."

"Here comes Bud now," said Porter. The boy handed several mimeographed sheets of paper to the professor, and the three newcomers climbed down into the dinghy.

Flipper, who had remained politely quiet throughout the conversation, stuck his head out of the water alongside the dinghy and began to chatter loudly.

"Well," said Dr. Avery, "who have we here?"

"That's Flipper," Bud explained proudly. "He's our pet dolphin."

"You're lucky boys to have such a pet. The dolphin is one of the noblest creatures of the sea—indeed, of the entire earth. Hello, Flipper."

Flipper jerked his head up and down in a greeting to the professor. Mel Latham, grumbling at the additional delay, picked up one of the oars from the bottom of the dinghy and prodded Flipper away.

"Come on! Get out of the way!" he growled.

"Hey!" Bud and Sandy yelled in unison. "You leave Flipper alone!"

But Flipper did not need anyone to help him. Before the words were out of the boys' mouths, the dolphin took the blade of the oar in his teeth and, with a powerful swirl of his flukes, backed away.

Mel Latham, standing in the stern of the small boat, was caught completely by surprise. "What in the . . ." he yelled, and, off balance, he teetered for a moment and then fell headlong into the lagoon.

"That's what I've been wanting to do all morning!" Jack Finch said laughingly. "I think old Mel got up on the wrong side of the bunk this morning."

Latham, spluttering with his mouth full of water, splashed back to the dock and climbed up the ladder. He stood for a moment, water dripping from him, and threw a dark look at Flipper. The dolphin tossed his head and gave what sounded like a raucous laugh.

Everyone else, including Dr. Avery, seemed to think the incident was amusing, and after a while a sheepish grin crossed the big man's swarthy features. He smoothed his moustache with the back of his hand. "I guess I got what I was asking for."

"Bud," Porter said, "run up to the house and get Mr. Latham a dry towel."

"Never mind that," Latham said. He climbed back down into the dinghy with water squishing out of his shoes. "I'll dry off when we get aboard the 'Shark.' That is, if we ever get there."

"Looks like a good dunking was all you needed, pal," said Jack Finch, grinning at his shipmate. He took a pack of cigarettes from his pocket and offered one to Latham. "Here, I'll light it for you."

"See, Mr. Latham?" Bud said proudly. "A dolphin's a pretty smart fellow after all." He glanced toward the black schooner riding smoothly at anchor across the lagoon and, with a sly grin, added, "The fact is, a dolphin can handle a shark any day of the week. And twice on Sunday!"

"You're absolutely correct, young man," agreed Dr. Avery. He turned back to the dripping Latham. "And now, Mel, we'd better get back to the ship and get to work, eh?"

"Sure, Professor," the big man said. He gave the starter cord a yank, and the dinghy moved away, circling. Just as it straightened and began to pick up speed, Flipper poked his head up a few feet behind the outboard motor and made a loud squeaking sound. Mel Latham looked around quickly, and just as he did, a perfectly aimed squirt of water caught him squarely between the eyes, to the boys' delight.

"Flipper!" Porter yelled. But the boys and Flipper were all laughing wildly as Latham hunched angrily at the motor and opened the throttle.

The little boat skimmed across the water toward the anchored schooner.

"You boys should teach that pet of yours some

manners," Porter said, trying to keep from smiling himself.

"Somebody better teach that Mr. Latham some manners," Bud said in defense of Flipper. "He started it."

"Sure, but enough is enough." Porter turned away and clapped both boys on their backs. "All right, men! We've had our little laugh; now let's get moving. We've got chores to do!"

"Aw, Dad," Bud complained, as expected. "Can't we play ball with Flipper for a little while first? All that old stuff can wait!"

"And maybe all that old stuff just won't get done at all? There's an old saying, Bud, that goes like this: 'Business before pleasure.' Now, then, let's get cracking!"

Bud scuffed his feet on the rough planking of the dock and looked longingly out at Flipper, who was tail-walking up and down alongside the dock.

"How come you've always got some old saying that takes all the fun out of life, Dad? You know, I sometimes think dolphins are a lot smarter than people are. You don't see them washing dishes or sweeping floors." He looked around at his father and scowled. "And you never hear them repeating any old saying, either!"

2. On Board

The first day the "Shark" was anchored in the lagoon at Coral Key was something of a disappointment for the Ricks boys. The professor and Jack Finch had seemed friendly enough, even if Mel Latham hadn't, and Bud and Sandy had hoped that they might be invited aboard the schooner to have a look around.

But Dr. Avery remained below deck most of the day, and Finch and Latham busied themselves at various tasks about the boat. They appeared to have no time for social calls.

Sandy was the first one down to the dock early the next morning. Bud came quickly down from the house, yawning and scratching his head. The smell of bacon frying in the kitchen almost turned him around, but he went on, his nose twitching.

"Anything going on out there?" he asked his brother when he got to the dock.

Sandy shook his head. "Nobody seems to be up yet. It's still early, though. Not quite six o'clock." He took his attention off the schooner long enough to look around at his brother. "Say, I thought this was your morning to fix breakfast."

"I thought it was yours," Bud countered. "I guess Dad's doing it, huh?"

"I suppose so." Both boys again looked toward the schooner across the calm lagoon. "You hear that little motor running out there?" Sandy said. "I think it's been going ever since they got here."

Bud cocked his head. He had heard it but had paid no particular attention to it. "Yeah. I wonder what it is," he said. The steady put-put of a gasoline engine echoed clearly across the water.

Porter Ricks walked down and joined the boys at the dock. "The engine? It's probably a generator," he said. "They need electricity aboard a boat like that, and when they're away from dockside electric plug-ins, they have to make their own electricity. And now that that's cleared up, how about you two gentlemen of leisure joining me for breakfast."

"Gentlemen of *what?*" puzzled Bud.

"It wasn't me goofing off, Dad," Sandy protested. "It's his turn to fix breakfast." He looked askance at his brother. "And by 'gentlemen of leisure,' Dad means goldbricks."

"What's a goldbrick?"

"Never mind!" said Sandy in disgust, and they all marched up to the house.

Breakfast done and the dishes washed once more, Bud wandered back outside to join Sandy. There were now signs of life aboard the "Shark." Wisps of smoke drifted up from the Charley Noble—the small chimney above the ship's galley. The companionway hatch opened and Mel Latham came on deck. He scratched his broad chest slowly with both hands and looked toward the shore, his mouth open in a wide yawn.

Jack Finch followed him on deck a few moments later and both men busied themselves at a hatch just aft of the helm. Finch then pulled the dinghy alongside the schooner and together they lowered something into the small boat.

"I wonder what they're doing," said Bud. "Say! What do you think of our going out there in the skiff and asking if there's something we can do?"

"I'd like to," Sandy replied, glancing at his watch.

"The trouble is, I told Dad I'd go down to the south camp area and take care of a few things."

Bud grinned tauntingly. "Dad, my foot! You're going down there so you can hang around that girl whose family is camping there!"

"Ask Dad yourself, stupid! He told me to pick up the trash and make sure the picnic tables and grills are clean and—well, that's why I'm going. Sally Aldridge has nothing to do with it."

"So! You even know what her name is!" But Bud's attention was diverted back to the "Shark." "Hey! There's the professor. They're all getting into the dinghy."

The small boat pulled away from the schooner and cut smartly across the lagoon toward the dock. Both boys were on hand to greet it, curious about the cargo. The dinghy eased alongside the dock, and Jack Finch leaped ashore. He took a small motor scooter that Mel Latham lifted from the boat, and deposited it on the dock.

The professor stepped ashore. "Good morning, boys. Is your father about?"

"Yes, sir," Bud answered, his eyes riveted on the scooter. "He's in the house. Want me to get him for you?"

"Never mind, Bud. I'll just walk up."

With great curiosity, the boys examined the small scooter. "This is really neat, huh?" Bud said, grinning. "I wonder how much one of these costs. Do you know, Mr. Latham?"

"Nope," the big man grunted.

"How about you, Mr. Finch?" Bud said, determined to have a price set.

"I'm afraid that's something I don't know," he said. "It's a handy little gadget, though. Easy to stow aboard ship, light, and just the thing for getting about on shore."

"Are you going to ride it now? How do you start it?"

"Well," Finch said, squatting beside the little machine, "you see this thing right here? That's the throttle, and you just set it so—"

"Belay it, Jack," muttered Latham.

"I was just showing the kid about the scooter, Mel."

"I said belay it. We got more to do than stand around gabbing with a kid. Anyhow, here comes the professor."

Dr. Avery and Porter Ricks walked down from the house, chatting amiably. ". . . I didn't think you'd have any objection to our leaving the scooter ashore, Mr. Ricks," Avery was saying. "However, it's always wise to have such things understood. I make it a point never to take too much for granted. It's a sure way to wear out one's welcome." He stopped and spoke to Latham. "Go on into town, Mel. I don't think you'll have any difficulty finding the parts you need at a marine supply house or a boatyard."

"I'll be driving the pickup truck into town myself in a few minutes," Porter said. "If there's anything I can do for you, just speak up."

"That's very kind of you," said the professor. "But there are several errands that Mel has to attend to, and it may take some time."

The big fellow climbed aboard the scooter and started the engine. As he headed up the road toward town, Bud could not suppress a smile. The scooter seemed so small and the rider so large.

Dr. Avery chuckled. "Quite a sight, isn't it? But it's a surprisingly rugged piece of machinery. I've found it almost indispensible aboard the 'Shark.' "

"Ready to head back to the ship, Professor?" asked Jack Finch.

"Right. And thanks again, Mr. Ricks."

When the dinghy was once more on its way across the lagoon, Bud frowned. "I wonder why they won't ask us to have a look aboard their old schooner. I have never been on a boat that was going on a real expedition before." He scratched his head thoughtfully for a moment. "What do you suppose they're planning to do when they get to wherever they're going, Dad? Maybe hunting treasure or something?"

"Dr. Avery hasn't said anything about that to me. But keep your shirt on, Son. They'll be here for quite a while yet. You may get your chance."

"Maybe it's an archaeological expedition," Sandy said.

"Could be," his father agreed. "Well, I've got to be heading into town."

"And I'm off for the south camp area," Sandy said.

"Keep an eye on the place, Bud," Porter said.

"Sure, Dad." As his brother and father left, Bud bent his head. "An archaeo—archaeo— I wonder what that is."

At that moment Flipper poked his head up out of the water a few yards from the edge of the dock and let loose a stream of chatter that sounded very much like he was laughing at his young friend.

"Aw, quiet!" Bud growled. "You don't know what it means, either, wise guy!"

Bud did his chores about the house and spent some time tossing a ball for Flipper. Neither Sandy nor his father would be back before noon, and in the meantime Bud was unofficially in charge of the park. But after sitting with his legs dangling over the edge of the dock for quite a while, staring out at the black schooner, he decided that he would not be deserting his post if he got into the outboard skiff and motored across the lagoon. After all, it was only two or three hundred yards, and he could keep an eye on the house from that distance.

It was only a matter of a few minutes before he had talked himself into doing what he wanted to do, and with a look of complete innocence on his freckled face, Bud jumped down into the skiff, gave the outboard starter a couple of yanks, and cast off.

With Flipper swimming easily alongside, Bud cruised slowly out toward the "Shark." A white canvas awning had been rigged over the cockpit aft of the tall mainmast, and Dr. Avery was sitting there in the shade with a folded navigational chart in his hands and an expression of deep concentration on his bearded face. Jack Finch was nowhere to be seen. At least, Bud said to himself, Mel Latham wasn't there. He seemed to be the grumpy one of the group, and if there was a chance of being invited aboard, it would probably be more likely while Latham was gone.

He let the skiff idle to within fifty feet of the schooner. The ship was even bigger than it seemed from a distance, and Bud sat gazing up in awe at the intricate rigging. When Dr. Avery did not seem aware of his presence, Bud cleared his throat as noisily as he could and called out, "Hi, Dr. Avery!"

The professor lowered the chart. "Eh? What? Oh! Oh, it's you, young fellow!"

Flipper darted out of the water, completely clear of the lagoon, and flopped over with a splash.

"And your aquatic friend!" Dr. Avery added with a chuckle of amusement.

"My aqu— Oh, you mean Flipper." Bud scratched his cheek uneasily. "I—er—I was just out this way and I thought—I mean I wondered if maybe there was anything you might need done, like washing the dishes or mopping the decks or something."

The professor stood up and walked to the rail. "Come alongside, Bud."

"Of course, I don't want to horn in if you're busy, you understand. It's like I said, I was just sort of out this way. . . ."

The professor leaned over and took hold of the skiff's bowline. "Bud, the day that young boys like yourself lose their curiosity will be a dark day indeed for this tired old world. Now, then, step aboard and let me give you a conducted tour of the good ship 'Shark.' "

"Dr. Avery," said a voice behind the professor. It was Jack Finch, leaning on his forearms in the open companionway, a look of uncertainty on his face. "I don't know if Mel would like visitors coming aboard just now, especially since he's not here himself. Maybe you ought to wait until Mel gets back from town before you invite Bud aboard."

"Oh?" said the professor. "I didn't realize Latham had taken complete charge of the expedition. I was under the impression that he was simply the sailing master of the 'Shark.' "

"Well . . . sure, that's what he is. But with all our special equipment and everything, you know how Mel is."

"I do indeed know how Mel is. I also know the meaning of hospitality. Young Bud and his father and brother have extended us their hospitality, and I am now returning the courtesy."

Finch ran one hand over his short-clipped hair, still frowning. "That's all well and good, sir, but I really think we should wait for Mel." He threw a glance toward the dock and the house across the lagoon. There was no sign of life other than a forlorn pelican sitting atop one of the dock pilings.

"Don't concern yourself with it, Jack," Dr. Avery said. He turned his attention back to Bud, who had been listening with his usual curiosity to the brief exchange between the two men. "Come aboard, young man!"

Bud could feel Jack Finch's eyes boring into him, and he stammered, "I—I don't mind coming back later, Dr. Avery, if you'd rather I didn't—"

"Nonsense! Nonsense! You'd think we were a crew of bloody pirates to listen to Jack. Now, then, come aboard!"

Finch disappeared down the companionway and Bud took hold of the rail and pulled himself aboard the schooner. The vessel had the solid feel of dry land underfoot. There was none of the rocking the boy was accustomed to when getting into the skiff, or even boarding the park launch. He shaded his eyes with one hand and squinted up again into the maze of rigging in the two tall masts. He could easily imagine himself at the helm, a buccaneer captain running down some rich merchantman bound homeward from the Indies. He could see the flash of cutlasses in the sun and hear the shouts of his men as the distance between the two vessels grew smaller.

"Gee, she's really something, Dr. Avery!" he said.

"She does very well for our purposes. Let's go

below and I'll show you how we live here. Follow me, and watch your step down the companionway. The stairs are rather steep."

Bud kept close behind the professor. At the foot of the companionway stairs—which were indeed steep—Bud found himself in a neat and compact galley. There was a spotless sink and work area, with cabinets above and below, as well as a large refrigerator and freezer. Dr. Avery showed him how the stove was mounted so that it remained level even when the ship was heeled over under a stiff breeze.

"Good hot food is very important aboard a sailing vessel," he said, "especially when it's in a blow. So the cook has got to keep on the job."

Next, they went forward along a narrow corridor and the professor opened a door to the right.

"This is my cabin, Bud. Not as large as your bedroom, I daresay, but very comfortable once you get used to it."

The boy peered in with keen interest. It was a small cabin, but every inch seemed to have been put to use. There was a desk and some bookshelves against the forward bulkhead, with each shelf crammed to capacity with books. There was a narrow bunk across the cabin just beneath an open porthole.

"Gosh, Professor," Bud said. "Have you read *all* these books?"

Dr. Avery smiled. "I look into them from time to time."

They went on up the corridor. There were other doors leading off both sides of the passageway. They were all cabins similar to his, the professor told Bud. "We sailed here with a skeleton crew. Just Latham, Jack, and myself. But by the time we're ready to leave on the expedition, we'll have quite a few men aboard."

"Are you going treasure hunting?" Bud asked.

The professor did not reply at once; then he nodded. "That's part of our mission."

"Won't you need a cabin boy? School's out for the whole summer, and I wouldn't even want any pay."

Dr. Avery laughed. "I'm afraid we're all set on this particular expedition, young fellow. But I'll definitely keep you in mind in the future."

"You will?" Bud asked, his eyes popping. "You really mean it?"

"I'd have to check with your father, of course."

"Dad wouldn't mind . . . at least, I don't think he would." His face brightened. "Flipper could swim right along with us, too!"

"We'll see what the situation is next year." Dr.

Avery put his hand on the boy's shoulder. "You know, Bud, you remind me a great deal of my own son."

Bud looked up at him in surprise. "You've got a son? Why isn't he with you?"

"Oh, he's a grown man now. But it doesn't seem so long ago that he was daydreaming of faraway places, just as you are."

"He's not going on the expedition with you?"

The professor sighed strangely. "No. No, but I hope to see him before the summer is over." His whole mood seemed to change suddenly. He led Bud on through the schooner, pausing briefly at the forward end of the passageway. He nodded toward the closed door there. "That's the storage hold for much of our equipment. Jack Finch is working on something in there now, so we won't interrupt him."

Bud could hear the steady put-put of a gasoline engine behind the closed door. The professor noticed the look of curiosity on the boy's face and explained. "That's our power generator. We've also got a gasoline-powered air compressor for refilling our scuba-diving tanks. You see, on expeditions such as this one we're a long way from any ports where tanks can be refilled. Actually, the 'Shark' is as complete as a little city. Entirely self-contained."

As he followed the professor through the passageway and onto the deck, Bud said, "Gee, it must be neat going on expeditions!"

"It's not all fun, young fellow. In fact, mostly it's hard work, and sometimes things get a bit nasty."

Flipper was cruising along back and forth beside the schooner waiting for Bud to get back in the skiff. The professor said, "I'm afraid I've nothing to offer your friend out there, Bud, but what would you say to a glass of lemonade and a piece of cake?"

"I'd say that sounds great!" Bud said truthfully, a big grin on his face.

The professor went down into the galley, and Bud walked to the big, spoked wheel in the cockpit. He took hold of it with both hands and, with his feet planted firmly on the deck, gave the wheel a turn. Well, he thought, even if he hadn't seen everything on the "Shark," he had at least gotten on board and seen some of it. That was a lot more than Sandy had done. He smiled to himself, thinking how nutty somebody had to be to go off to see some girl, when he could be on board a real expedition schooner instead.

"It's really something, Flipper," Bud explained to his pet when he had returned to the dock. "There are all sorts of cabins and doors and things below deck. Yes, sir, I'm going to go on an expedition with the professor one of these days on the 'Shark'!"

Flipper smacked the water with his flukes and jabbered something in reply. He bobbed his head up and down impatiently as Bud picked up a ball.

"Okay, fella, here goes!" He wound up and threw the ball out across the water as hard as he could. With a swirl of his powerful flukes, Flipper shot through the water, reaching the spot before the ball did and catching it neatly on his beak. He cocked his head sharply to one side and sent the ball hurtling back to Bud as accurately as a big-league pitcher putting a fast one right over the plate for a strike.

Bud was winding up to throw it again when he heard the sound of a motor on the road beyond the house. He turned to see the scooter bearing Mel Latham come around the bend and angle down toward the dock. The little machine seemed about to crumple beneath its weighty passenger. Latham pulled to a stop and lowered the kickstand.

"Hi, Mr. Latham," said Bud.

"Hello, sonny."

"Say, do you want me to run you out to the 'Shark' in our skiff?"

The big fellow shook his head. "I'll just whistle for Finch."

"It's no trouble. Besides, I'm not busy right now. I've got to go out with Dad after lunch to check where he thinks some poachers have been setting lobster pots, but till then I could help you if you want me to. I'm pretty good at mopping and—"

The darkly tanned face seemed to grow even darker behind the heavy moustache. "You say your old man's going checking for poachers, huh? What's that all about? Where does he do this checking?"

"Well," Bud said, "you probably know it's against the law to do any lobstering inside the marine preserve, the same as spearfishing and wreck salvaging and some other things—"

"Yeah, yeah," Mel Latham said impatiently. "I know all about that. But just where is it your old man does this checking for lobster pots?"

Why was he so interested in that? Bud asked himself. Fleetingly, it occurred to him that perhaps he had already talked too much. Suppose that Latham himself was a poacher? But even as the thought went through his mind he knew that it was silly. Nobody with a fine schooner like the "Shark" would fool around with poaching.

"It's somewhere down at the south end of the preserve. It's a real good place for lobsters, and Dad has to run poachers off all the time. At least, I think that's where we're going."

Latham nodded, and some of the concern seemed to leave his expression. He went to the end of the dock, stuck two fingers in his mouth, and blew. A shrill whistle split the air. Across the lagoon, Dr. Avery looked up from his reading beneath the awning, and a moment later Jack Finch came on deck, jumped down into the dinghy, and set out for shore.

Bud ambled back to the edge and sat down, dangling his legs over, and halfheartedly tossed the ball out to Flipper.

3. Disappearance

Dr. Charles Avery and his two companions kept themselves occupied aboard the schooner "Shark" for the next several days. Occasionally, either Jack Finch or Mel Latham came ashore to go into town on the scooter for some supply or piece of equipment that they needed. Dr. Avery came ashore once and visited briefly with Porter Ricks and the boys.

It was on the fourth day after the arrival of the "Shark" that the professor came ashore with a chart of the marine preserve. He unrolled the chart on the porch table. "I plan to do a bit of diving at the wreck of the 'El Capitan,' Mr. Ricks." He indicated a spot on the chart. "I know it's in this general area, but I thought you might pinpoint it for me."

"The old Spanish galleon on Hawk Reef?" asked

Sandy, bending over to examine the paper.

"That's right," the professor said, nodding.

"You've got the right place there, Dr. Avery," Porter Ricks said. "But the old girl has been there close to three hundred years and there isn't much left to see." He smoothed the chart. "I suppose the only reason there's any sign of it at all is that apparently she slipped over the reef right here"—he marked an ✕ on the chart—"and settled to the bottom between the reef and the shore. The water is calm there, with little surf or current."

Dr. Avery pursed his lips and nodded. "It's not more than half a mile up the bay from the lagoon, either. Very handy."

"Isn't the 'El Capitan' one of the wrecks you wrote about in your book, sir?" Sandy inquired.

"The name *El Capitan* was a popular one for Spanish ships in those days. There are several wrecks by that name along the coast here and in the Bahama Islands. But you're right, Sandy. I did include this particular shipwreck in the book. It took place during a severe storm, probably one of the tropical storms which we call hurricanes today. Of course, in those days they had no accurate way of forecasting weather, and ships were often caught in storms while at sea. The fury of the wind would drive them off course and many wound up crashing on reefs, just as the 'El Capitan' did."

"What do you think happened to all that gold, Dr. Avery?" Sandy asked.

Bud's ears perked up. "Gold? All what gold?"

Porter Ricks said, "The 'El Capitan' was supposedly taking a shipment of gold from Mexico, bound for Spain."

"From old records I've seen, it would probably be valued at up to two million dollars at present gold prices," Dr. Avery put in.

Bud gave a whistle. "Two million dollars! *Wow!*"

The professor continued, "The Spaniards did quite a lot of salvaging on many of their wrecked ships, more than most people realize. And they did very well, considering they had none of the equipment we have for diving today. If you've ever tried to have a look underwater without the benefit of a diving mask, you can appreciate at least one problem they had to face. My guess on this particular wreck is that they salvaged their gold, especially since the galleon lay in protected and relatively shallow water."

"I suppose so," Porter said. "I've never heard of any gold being found on the wreck, even before the area was designated a preserve."

"Can we come along with you, Dr. Avery?" Bud asked excitedly.

"Whoa, now, fella!" chided his father. "You know better than to go inviting yourself along. Besides, you and Sandy have dived on the old wreck dozens of times."

"Sure, Dad," Bud said, "but not with anybody like Dr. Avery."

"It's perfectly all right, Mr. Ricks," said the professor. "The fact is, I'd rather enjoy having the boys along. I'd also like to see that pet dolphin of yours. I've done a bit of research on dolphins and other cetaceans. As you probably know, there has been some fascinating work done in this field in recent years, especially the work of Dr. Lilly in the Virgin Islands."

"Flipper's a cet—ceta—whatever it was you said?" Bud frowned.

The professor grinned and nodded. "That's right, young fellow. But don't hold it against Flipper. He didn't choose the name. Cetaceans, you know, are among the more intelligent creatures of our earth."

"Then it's okay if we go along on the dive, sir?" Sandy asked. "We could take our skiff. That would help with the diving gear."

"When are you going, Professor?" Bud said.

Dr. Avery rubbed his beard for a moment. "What about tomorrow morning? Jack Finch plans to test one or two pieces of our diving equipment this afternoon. Yes, I think tomorrow morning would be fine. How about you, Mr. Ricks? Would you care to join us?"

"Thanks, Dr. Avery, but I'm afraid I can't make it. I've got some reports to write and a few things to see to around the park. There's a bit more to being a ranger than meets the eye. However, I'm sure the boys will get a big kick out of going along. They're both qualified scuba divers, and they have their own equipment."

"Well," said the professor as he rolled up his chart, "I'll see you lads at about seven tomorrow morning."

"Gosh!" Bud marveled as he watched the professor head back out toward the "Shark." "Just think, going diving with a real expedition scientist!"

The sun had dropped below the tops of the tall palms behind the Rickses' house, and the breeze had vanished almost entirely. Sitting quietly on a dock piling, the old bird the boys called Pelican Pete stared at the lagoon. The surface of the water was like a mirror except for the smooth waves set in motion by Flipper as he rushed in toward the dock. He came up out of the water on his flukes, jabbered at Bud who was sitting on the edge of the dock, and flopped over with a big splash.

Sandy walked down from the house. "What's eating him?" he asked.

"You noticed it, too, huh? Gee, I don't know what it is. It seems like just about every day this time he comes over here, then swims back out around the 'Shark,' and comes back to start yakking like crazy. See? There he goes!"

With his dorsal fin cutting the water, Flipper sped out toward the schooner. He circled the vessel, then, just as Bud had said, came zipping back to the dock and began to squawk and jabber.

"Hey!" Bud said, a smile spreading across his freckled face. "Do you suppose he just doesn't like sharks? Get it? The name of the schooner is the—"

"I get it," Sandy groaned, shaking his head. "And it isn't funny. Say, where's their dinghy?"

"The dinghy? Oh, I saw Jack Finch crank it up two or three hours ago. He loaded some diving gear in it and headed down the bay. It's going to be sunset before long. Seems like he ought to be getting back."

Inside the house the telephone began to ring. "Is

Dad up there?" asked Bud.

"No. I'll get it." Sandy trotted up the slope and went into the house.

Bud took another quizzical look at Flipper, who was still acting strangely, then followed Sandy to the house. He found his brother listening intently to someone on the telephone.

"Yes, sir," Sandy said after a few moments. "That sounds like their dinghy all right. Hold on just a second. I'll check with Bud." He lowered the phone. "Was anybody else with Mr. Finch when you saw him leave in the dinghy, Bud?"

"Nope," he said. "He was all by himself, and like I said before, he had some scuba stuff with him. Who wants to know? Did something happen?"

"It's Lieutenant Bentley at the Coast Guard station. Some kids out water-skiing found the dinghy drifting on the bay about three miles south of here. It was empty."

He lifted the phone again and repeated what Bud had told him. Then he said, "Dad should be back before long. I'll have him phone you as soon as he comes in." He listened again for several moments. "All right, sir, we'll do that instead. Good-bye."

"Something's happened to Mr. Finch!" Bud exclaimed. "What——"

"Look, we've got to get busy. I'm going out in the jeep to try to locate Dad. You take the skiff and go out to the 'Shark.' Tell Dr. Avery and Mr. Latham that the lieutenant is on his way over here in a Coast Guard boat. He'll meet them here at the house."

"What'll I tell 'em?"

"Tell them just what we know—that the dinghy's been found adrift, and something may have happened to Jack Finch. Get going! Lieutenant Bentley's already on his way!"

Fifteen minutes later a gleaming white picket boat lay alongside the park dock, just aft of the launch. While two Coastguardsmen waited on board, Lt. Ed Bentley briefed the group on the dock.

"It sounds bad, I'm afraid," he said. "The kids who found the boat said that when they first saw it about a quarter of a mile from where they were skiing, there was a tall, black, triangular thing circling around the dinghy. The older boy, the one who was operating the ski boat, says he's pretty certain it was at least five feet out of the water, judging by a comparison with the dinghy at that distance."

"Good heavens!" exclaimed Dr. Avery. "Lieutenant, do you know what that sounds like? Could it possibly have been a killer whale?"

"A *killer whale?*" Porter Ricks queried anxiously. "Here at Coral Key? I've never heard of one being seen around here."

"I don't know of anything else that would match that description, do you?" the lieutenant said. He turned toward the professor. "I've got two boats in the area now, but there has been absolutely no sign of Finch. And there was no diving equipment in the boat when it was found. Apparently he was diving near one of the small islands down there."

"Wasn't his anchor out?" Porter asked.

"No. Maybe he was just taking a look near the boat. There was no wind, and so he may have figured it would be safe enough."

"What about these people who claim to have seen this—this fin?" Dr. Avery said. "Do you think they are reliable? I mean, is there any possibility of a hoax?"

"None," Lieutenant Bentley said without hesitation. "They're all young people who live around here. They're not the prankster type."

The professor rubbed the back of one hand across his eyes. "I—I can't believe it! It doesn't seem possible such a thing could happen. Why, I've known young Finch for years!"

Mel Latham spoke up for the first time. "I've seen

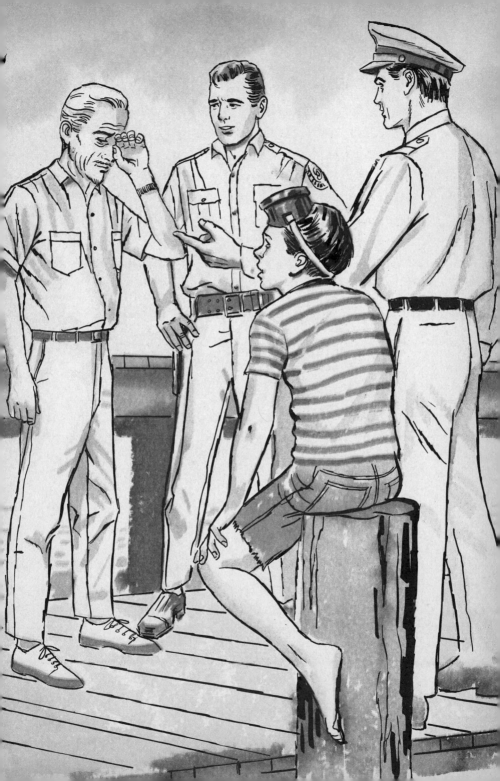

the devils in action. I was first mate aboard a tramp freighter off the coast of Alaska back in 'forty-nine. We came on a pack of killer whales that had squared off against a big baleen whale. Four of 'em were holding him port and starboard by his flippers, and all the rest were prying open his mouth to get at the tongue, which I've heard the old-timers say is a favorite snack of killer whales. Well, we hove the ship to, to watch. It seemed that the whole pack was taking orders from a big bull killer who stayed off to one side of the carnage the whole time. They took what they wanted and left the big baleen to die, or for the sharks to finish off. I can tell you first-hand, they are as fearsome a creature as lives on this earth. It can make a man stay awake nights just thinking of it."

"What Mel says is true, of course," Dr. Avery agreed. "Stories of killer whales are some of the most bloodcurdling I've ever heard. They seem to be one of the few creatures in nature—other than man himself—that kills for the sheer pleasure of it."

"But—but what about Mr. Finch?" Bud asked.

"We'll continue the search," Lieutenant Bentley said. "It'll be dark in another half an hour, but we'll keep all the boats we can out through the night, and I've got a couple of helicopters coming down from

the Dinner Key base at first light in the morning.
That is, if nothing's turned up by then."

Mel Latham gave his head a shake. "If it was a
killer out there, there ain't no use in looking for
Jack."

Lieutenant Bentley headed for the boat. "We'll
keep looking."

"I'll take the park launch and join you," Porter
Ricks said.

"I'd like to come," said the professor firmly.

"There's plenty of room in the launch," Porter
said. "Hop in."

"A—a killer whale!" breathed Bud, his eyes wide.
"Right here in the bay!" And suddenly he remembered the strange way Flipper had been acting lately,
and he wondered if this had anything to do with it.

The Coast Guard boats and the park launch
fanned out in a search pattern across the bay in the
area where the dinghy had been abandoned. They
searched until long after dark, their lights crisscross-
ing over the surface. But not the slightest trace of
Jack Finch was found.

It was Mel Latham who put it into words as the
park launch pulled back into the dock close to midnight. "Jack's had it. The devilish beast got him.

It couldn't be anything else."

"But a—a killer whale—here!" Sandy said, disbelief on his face.

"The entire sea, from pole to pole, is their cruising ground, young man," Dr. Avery explained. "And it is a well-established fact that they prefer warm-blooded prey, such as seals, large and small whales of other species, dolphins, perhaps even man—"

"*Dolphins?*" gasped Bud.

The professor nodded. "Yes, I'm afraid so. In fact, it is one of their favorite foods."

"Golly! What about Flipper, Dad?" Bud said, greatly concerned over the safety of his pet.

As if to join in the discussion, Flipper himself poked his head up from the dark waters of the lagoon in the circle of light from the boat and the dock light, and he began to jabber away.

"I'd say Flipper doesn't seem very worried about killer whales or anything else," Porter Ricks said, putting one arm around Bud's shoulders.

"Neither was Mr. Finch," Bud said, "until. . . ."

The radio receiver crackled and Lieutenant Bentley's voice came over the speaker. "Coast Guard one-three-four to Ranger Porter Ricks. Over."

Porter lifted the microphone and pressed the button. "Ricks to Coast Guard one-three-four. Over."

"Porter, we'll resume the search at daybreak, and we'd appreciate your joining in. Sleep well. Coast Guard one-three-four, out."

Of course, the planned dive at the wreck of the "El Capitan" was called off next morning. The headline on the front page of the *Coral Key Gazette* read in big letters: DIVER MISSING—KILLER WHALE IN BAY AREA. The news was also broadcast on all radio stations.

Official warnings were issued by the Coast Guard for divers, swimmers, water skiers, and everyone else to stay out of the water until it could be positively determined if the missing man had been attacked by a killer whale, and if the killer was still in the area.

The morning search produced no clue to Jack Finch's fate, but as the day progressed calls began to come in from various places that the black fin had been sighted. Carloads of curious people drove into the park to see the schooner that the ill-fated diver had arrived on.

At midafternoon Mel Latham and Dr. Avery came across the lagoon and went up the slope to the Rickses' house. Bud met them at the door.

"Is your father here?" the professor asked wearily.

"He's talking to the parks commissioner on the

telephone, I think. Just have a seat out here on the porch and I'll tell him you're here."

The two men dropped down into chairs. Latham lit a cigarette and leaned back to wait, gazing at the sparkling waters of the bay outside the lagoon. Almost fifteen minutes dragged by before Porter joined them.

"I'm sorry I kept you waiting so long," he said. "The commissioner couldn't believe what's happened, and frankly I still find it pretty difficult myself."

"You mean you don't think there's a killer whale in the bay?" the professor asked.

Porter sighed and shook his head. "I suppose I'll have to believe it. There have been nearly a dozen phone calls to the Coast Guard already today. People claim to have seen the thing all over the bay area. Some of it might be a sort of mass hysteria, but I don't doubt some of these people have seen something." Porter walked across the porch, his hands clasped behind him.

"As for us," Dr. Avery said, "it's necessary to be realistic. Jack is dead, we're convinced of that. I'll take care of notifying the proper people. Actually, the boy hadn't much family, so there'll be no difficulty there. There's a brother whom he hadn't seen in many years, and that's about the extent of it." He rubbed his beard for a moment. "As for the expedition, I'm afraid this is something of a setback. Jack was a key diver. He had been with me on previous expeditions of this sort, and now he must be replaced. I hope it won't be an inconvenience to you to have us stay here longer than we originally expected."

Porter turned and looked at the two men. Strangely, it had occurred to him that what had happened might do just the opposite. "Stay as long as you wish. But it still seems to me the inconvenience is not mine, but yours."

The professor shrugged his shoulders. "If that becomes the case, of course, we'll move on. However, I much prefer a quiet and remote anchorage such as this to the hustle and bustle of a crowded boatyard. And especially now, I'm afraid the 'Shark' would become the target of curiosity seekers."

"Well, I hope it works out," Porter Ricks said.

Bud walked out and down to the dock. Out in the lagoon he could see Flipper cruising idly about. He wished vainly that there was someplace to keep Flipper until they were certain the killer whale had moved on. The funny thing about it was that Flipper himself didn't seem concerned at all. Maybe, Bud thought, he just didn't know what had happened.

4. Bad News for Flipper

Next morning Bud went into town with his father. Almost before the pickup truck had come to a stop in front of Peeler's Hardware Store, where Porter Ricks had to pick up some supplies, young Hank Peeler dashed up to the truck and was firing questions at them. Hank was nearly eleven years old, a schoolmate of Bud's as well as one of his best friends.

"Did you see the killer whale? How big was he? Did he really eat that fella up the way everybody says?"

Bud shook his head. "We didn't see the killer whale, Hank, but some other folks did. He's out there in the bay someplace, you can bet on that."

"Now, hold your horses, Son. We're not sure he's still in the area," his father reminded him.

"Well . . . maybe not," Bud said, reluctant to let an exciting story be watered down. His face brightened. "But we don't know that he *ain't* around here, either!"

"Isn't," corrected his father, opening the door and stepping down. "And you're right, we really don't know one way or the other. That's why I want you boys to stay out of the water until we *do* know." He turned to the other boy. "Is your dad inside, Hank?"

"Yes, sir."

Porter Ricks went into the store, while Hank continued to level a barrage of questions at his friend. "What's the boat like, Bud? The one the guy came here on."

"It's a big black schooner named the 'Shark,' and it's taking them on a real expedition as soon as they can get somebody to take Mr. Finch's place. They're going looking for treasure and all sorts of things. The professor—that's Dr. Charles Avery—is in charge of it. At least, I think he is. Anyhow, now that Jack Finch got eaten up by the killer whale, they're going to have to stick around Coral Key longer than they figured."

Hank whistled softly. "Gee, *eaten up*. It sounds real terrible, you know?"

Bud's eyebrows shot up. "My gosh, Hank, it *is*

real terrible! It's *horrible,* in fact."

"What about Flipper? Do killer whales and dolphins get along together?"

Bud would have been satisfied if Hank hadn't brought that up. He had stayed awake far into the night worrying about just that. He frowned and scratched his head. "I—I don't think so. The professor says that killer whales would rather eat dolphins than almost anything else. But Flipper's smart! He's real smart! He can look after himself. . . ." He slumped back against the side of the truck. "I hope."

The tiny motor scooter bearing Mel Latham came popping around the corner and pulled to a stop beside the two boys.

"Good morning, Mr. Latham," Bud said.

The big man dismounted and nodded. "Hi, sonny. I guess your old man's inside the store, huh?"

"Yes, sir. Want me to get him for you?"

"I've got to go in. I thought I might get him to haul some stuff back to the dock for me in the truck. This scooter's okay for getting around, but it ain't much for hauling cargo."

The moment Latham disappeared through the door, Hank turned toward Bud. "Is that one of the men from the 'Shark'?"

"Yeah. That's Mel Latham. I heard the professor

say that he is the sailing master of the schooner, whatever that is."

"Maybe it's something like a captain," Hank suggested. "Whatever it is, he sure looks tough. Like a pirate or something."

Bud laughed. "You should have seen Flipper when Mr. Latham got tough with him. Flipper pulled him right out of the boat into the lagoon!" He recounted to his friend the incident of the first day. "Then," Bud went on, his eyes twinkling, "when they started back to the schooner in their dinghy, Flipper gave him a squirt of water right between the eyes. You should have seen it! Even Dad could hardly keep from busting out laughing!"

The two boys shrieked with laughter until tears ran down their cheeks. When he was able to speak, Hank said, "How about if I come out to your house today, Bud? I could ride my bike out in about an hour."

"Sure, come on out. Maybe I can even get Dr. Avery to let you have a look on board the 'Shark.' "

Hank's eyes popped. "Boy! You really think he would?"

"Maybe. Right now I better get inside and help Dad."

At that moment Porter Ricks and Mel Latham

came out of the store, both carrying boxes. Latham tossed his in the truck bed and climbed once more onto the scooter. "Just leave 'em on the dock, Ranger. The professor'll pick 'em up."

"Sure thing," Porter said. "By the way, did either of you talk to Lieutenant Bentley this morning?"

"We called him on the ship-to-shore radio just before I left. He said they would keep the boats out on the bay this morning, but that it would be routine. He doesn't hold out any hope for poor Jack, and neither do we. Too bad. He was a good boy. I'm gonna miss him." He shook his head, smoothed his bushy moustache, and started the scooter. "Well, gotta get moving."

Bud Ricks and his father had several more errands to attend to in town, and everywhere it was the same: They were deluged with questions about the killer whale and the missing diver from the schooner. It was nearly noon when they headed out the road toward Coral Key Park, and Bud's stomach was already sending up urgent messages inquiring about lunch. But Bud was far too excited about all that was happening to let hunger interfere.

As they drove along, Bud said, "How come killer whales can't just eat fish, Dad? Why do they have to like dolphins? I don't understand."

"I'm afraid I haven't got the answer to that one, Son," he replied. "Maybe they're something like we are. Can you imagine how dull eating would be if you ate fish for every meal?"

They reached the house and drove around to the dock. The "Shark's" dinghy was tied up alongside the skiff, and Dr. Avery was standing at the edge of the dock, watching Flipper.

"Do you ever get the feeling that this creature is looking on you with a definite air of superiority?" he said to Porter with a smile.

"Quite often." Porter grinned. "Bud, get that stuff out of the back of the truck for Dr. Avery."

The professor walked to the truck. "Good. Mel hasn't returned yet, and I'm glad he happened to see you in town. There are a few things I need here." He lifted the boxes out, then paused. "By the way, Lieutenant Bentley dropped by in the picket boat about half an hour ago. He wanted to check with me before he called off the search for Jack Finch. We both agreed that it was futile. If the boy were alive, he would have turned up by now."

"I'm afraid I'll have to agree with you," Porter said.

"Was anybody out here looking for me?" Bud said,

remembering that Hank had planned to come out.

"I did see a young fellow on a bicycle earlier. Your brother was here, and the two of them went down the road in that direction." He pointed toward the south camp area.

"Thank you, sir," Bud said and went to the end of the dock. Flipper spied him, raced past the dock, and shot up into the air in an acrobatic display. He swam slowly to the dock and jabbered up at the boy.

"He sure doesn't seem worried about any old killer whale. Professor . . ." Bud said tentatively, "is it *really* true that killer whales eat dolphins?"

The professor stroked his beard for a moment, looked sidelong at Porter Ricks, then said, "I'm afraid so, Bud. But I wouldn't worry about Flipper."

"How do they know killer whales eat dolphins? I mean, has anybody ever seen one of 'em eating a dolphin?" Bud leaned over and patted Flipper's gleaming head.

"I couldn't actually say it's been seen. But there is considerable evidence. Some years ago an orca— that's the scientific name for the killer—was taken by whalers, and his carcass was opened. The bodies of thirteen dolphins and fourteen seals were found in his stomach."

Bud's face whitened and his mouth dropped open in alarm. "Thir*teen* . . . like—like Flipper?"

"I feel confident that your friend there can look after himself." The professor was obviously not pleased with himself for having stirred the deep concern in the youngster. "Jack Finch was simply very unlucky to be at the wrong place at the wrong time."

He glanced at his watch and then up toward the road. "I wonder what's keeping Latham."

His question was answered at once by the high-pitched popping of the scooter, and moments later it came easing around the house and down to the dock. Latham swung off the little machine. "Ready to shove off, Professor?"

The scientist nodded. Porter Ricks watched him with interest. Something seemed to be bothering him, something that had not shown the previous day, even when the news of Jack Finch's probable fate had reached him.

On an impulse Porter said, "Dr. Avery, what about you and Mr. Latham having dinner ashore with us tonight? Might do you both some good to get off the ship for an evening after all that's happened. I can't promise you anything fancy, but we'd like very much to have you join us."

"No, thanks," Latham said.

"Nonsense!" Dr. Avery broke in. "We'd be delighted. At least, *I* would. How about you, Mel? Pleasant company and a change of cooking would do us both a world of good."

The big fellow looked at the professor with a strange expression. "We've got work to do tonight; you know that."

"Yes——" He seemed to hesitate, and then the smile returned. "But the work can wait."

Latham shrugged slightly and looked around at Porter. "Okay."

"About eight o'clock suit you?" said Porter.

"Sounds fine," the professor said.

Not long after Mel Latham and the professor had returned to the "Shark," Sandy and young Hank Peeler came back from the south camp area. Both boys were finishing off a piece of chocolate cake as they came out onto the dock.

"Boy, oh, boy!" Hank exclaimed, licking his fingers. "That Mrs. Aldridge can really make a cake!"

"Sally's mother?" Bud inquired. "Sandy's girl friend's mother?"

"She's not my girl friend," his older brother said, "but it's not a bad idea, especially after eating that cake."

"Can we go out to the 'Shark'?" Hank wanted to

know. He gazed admiringly out at the black schooner lying in the sparkling lagoon. "Boy, that's really some boat, isn't it?"

Porter Ricks, who had been doing some thinking about the strange behavior of the professor, said, "You boys leave them alone this afternoon. They'll be here for supper. Maybe you can get Dr. Avery to ask you aboard tomorrow."

"Can Hank eat with us?" Bud said.

Porter grinned and rumpled his son's hair. "Sure. One more mouth—even Hank's—won't sink us!"

"Oh, I almost forgot something, Dad," Sandy put in. "Sally's father, Mr. Aldridge, said he might drop around later to have a word with you. He saw something out on the bay a few nights ago. He wasn't sure then, but now he thinks it could have been the killer whale."

"There've been quite a few reports today already."

At eight o'clock that evening the little dinghy came purring across the lagoon. Porter Ricks had charcoal glowing in the grill when Latham and the professor came up from the dock.

"This is very neighborly of you and the boys, Mr. Ricks," said the professor, dropping down into a chair and accepting a tall glass of iced tea from the tray Bud brought out of the house.

"Hamburgers, beans, and a salad," said Porter. "Nothing fancy, but the boys seem to be thriving on it, so it shouldn't do us any harm."

"I've been listening to your local radio station this evening," said the professor. "All this is causing quite a stir."

"Yeah," Bud grumbled, scuffing his foot at the ground. "Nobody can even go in swimming now. I almost died from the heat today!"

"Come on, Son," Porter laughed. "You're spreading it on a bit thick, aren't you? Besides, if it's that hot, why don't you go take a nice cold shower?"

"A shower? A—a *bath?* I may be dying, Dad, but I'm not crazy!"

Sandy pulled a chair alongside Dr. Avery's. "Do killer whales usually hang around a place for long, sir?"

"That's not an easy question to answer, Sandy." The professor rubbed his hands together and pursed his lips. "I would suppose that depended on a number of things."

"What the professor means," put in Mel Latham, "is that there ain't any way of knowing for sure, and it's best to be on the safe side. They're as peculiar as they are ornery, and that's plenty."

"I read someplace that they're really a member of the dolphin family," Sandy said.

Bud's eyebrows shot up in astonishment. "I don't believe you!"

"It's true enough, Bud," Dr. Avery said with a nod. Then he smiled faintly at the worried boy. "But they're nothing like your friend out there in the lagoon. His side of the family got the good disposition and the sense of humor. Old man orca got a big streak of meanness."

"Well . . ." Bud hedged, "I'll still bet Flipper wouldn't claim kin to him."

Porter Ricks chuckled and put the hamburgers on the grill. The mouth-watering smell of the broiling beef took everyone's mind off the subject of killer whales, and the rest of the evening went along pleasantly.

Even so, when the visitors said good night at a bit past ten o'clock, Porter resolved to call Ed Bentley first thing tomorrow and do a little checking on the schooner "Shark" and her crew.

5. Bud the Beachcomber

During the week that followed, a number of additional reports were turned in by people who thought they had gotten a glimpse of something that might have been the killer whale. Several of them placed the sightings in the south part of the bay, which was inside the boundaries of the Coral Key Marine Preserve. Park Ranger Porter Ricks and his two sons checked these out, while those in other areas were examined by the Coast Guard. One turned out to be a floating log and another was a fishing skiff that had drifted out into the bay from a camp.

Porter dropped into Lt. Ed Bentley's office at the Coast Guard station on Friday morning. The officer was at his desk, a pipe clenched between his teeth. He motioned his friend into a chair beside the desk.

"What do you think, Porter?" he asked. "I mean, about these so-called sightings of the killer whale? Why is it *we* haven't seen the blasted thing? You want to know what this is beginning to remind me of? That flying saucer business of a few years ago when everybody and his brother was seeing spaceships and little green men. Everybody, that is, but the authorities who had to check out the things."

Porter grinned and sat down, tossing his cap on the desk. "Maybe that's what it is, Ed. But there's no doubt some of these people are seeing something. There's a family that's spending a month or so tenting at the south camp area in the park—folks by the name of Aldridge. Mr. Aldridge came around to see me a few days ago. Seems that one evening he was on the beach at the edge of the bay, just below the mouth of Coral Key lagoon, and he saw something two or three hundred yards out. Of course, it was dark, but there was a moon that night. The object was low in the water and moving slowly toward the lagoon. For a moment he thought it might be a small boat, but there was no sound of a motor, and he couldn't detect any movement such as might have been made by someone rowing. He says he lost sight of it shortly afterward. If this *were* the killer, it could simply have submerged, of course. Now, this fellow

Aldridge seems to be a pretty steady sort, not at all given to seeing things that aren't there. The fact is, I doubt if the man has ever seen a flying saucer."

The Coast Guard officer gave a short laugh. "I get your point. And, of course, something has obviously happened to this Jack Finch, so the killer whale story holds water. At this point I can't figure anything else, can you?"

"No, I can't," Porter replied. "And that's one reason I asked you to check on the 'Shark' and her crew. Have you heard anything yet?"

"Yes, something came in this morning. I was about to call you when you dropped in." He shuffled through a stack of papers on his desk and pulled out an envelope. "Here it is." He opened the envelope and removed several official-looking papers. "This is a copy of the 'Shark's' Coast Guard registration document. The schooner belongs to a nonprofit foundation which apparently is somehow connected with Northeastern Oceanographic University in Maine. Dr. Charles Avery is chief director of the foundation. The 'Shark' is used primarily for such things as oceanographic research, scientific exploration, and educational work. She is also chartered out to private individuals from time to time. It seems that Avery himself has chartered the schooner for the summer."

Porter Ricks pulled his chair around and looked over the documents. After a while he gave his chin a thoughtful rub. "I guess I was barking up the wrong tree," he said.

The lieutenant pushed the papers aside. "Just what tree were you barking up, Porter?"

"I don't really know. There's something about our visitors at Coral Key that I just can't quite put my finger on. For one thing, the fact that they *are* visitors at Coral Key is puzzling. They'd be much better off at a boatyard closer to town. And for another thing, Flipper's been acting very odd lately and it seems to have something to do with the schooner being in the lagoon."

Bentley leaned back in his chair and grinned. "Come on now, boy! Are you letting that trick dolphin do your thinking for you?"

Porter shrugged. "When it comes to what's beneath the water, Ed, I just might do that." He stood up and pushed the chair back. He looked down at the envelope again. "Did your report mention either Latham or Jack Finch?"

"Latham or Finch?" Bentley mused. Once more he thumbed through the papers. "I don't think so . . . wait. Here's something about Finch. Seems he was also a director of the foundation. It says here that he was a teaching assistant to Dr. Avery at the university."

Porter sighed. "Certainly nothing suspicious about that. What about Mel Latham?"

"Nothing on him," Bentley said with a shake of his head. "Of course, if they're planning on putting into foreign ports on this expedition, members of the crew would have to have official papers. If their work entailed any lengthy stays they'd need passports, immunization papers, that sort of thing. Also, if there is to be any salvage work in territorial waters of the Central American countries, they'd have to have permits from those countries."

A young Coast Guard yeoman got up from a teletype machine across the office and came to the desk. "Excuse me, Lieutenant Bentley, but the official weather advisory on that storm at sea has just come through. You said you wanted it right away. It's moving in a southeasterly direction at the present time, so there's no threat to our area unless it reverses course. Winds up to fifty knots." He placed the typed message on the desk.

"Thanks, Franklin."

"At least that's good news," Porter Ricks said. He picked up his cap. "Well, I'd better get back on the job. And thanks, Ed."

"Don't mention it. You're a taxpayer, aren't you?" He grinned. "It's you taxpayers that pay my salary."

Porter laughed. "And you're paying mine, so thanks. See you later."

Bud Ricks had put a couple of biscuits left over from breakfast into his pants' pockets, and while his father was at the Coast Guard station the boy took a walk along the beach from the dock toward the mouth of the lagoon and the bay shore. A dozen yards out from the beach Flipper swam along slowly, cocking an eye toward Bud from time to time and giving a squawk or two as if to ask his young friend what was going on.

At the point where the lagoon merged with the bay, Pelican Pete stood morosely on the sand at the edge of the water. He seemed to be weighing his hunger against the effort of flapping his wings and looking for food. The hunger won out, for he began to hop along, flexing his long wings until he was airborne. Then he banked out across the bay and started looking down for a likely fish for breakfast.

"Let's go around to the camp area, Flipper," Bud said, recalling the chocolate cake that Sandy and Hank had extolled so highly. The biscuits in his pockets would be a reserve against the chance that

Mrs. Aldridge was out of cake or failed to invite him to have a slice.

Flipper answered with a bob of his head. It was getting on Bud's nerves, seeing the fun Flipper was having in the cool, clear water, while Bud himself was not allowed to do more than get his feet wet. What harm could it do to take a quick swim? He stopped and, facing out toward the open water, put his hands on his hips. How long, he wondered, was this killer whale scare going to last? One thing was sure, it had certainly put a scare into most people. Usually, on a warm summer morning such as this, you could see at least one or two boats pulling water skiers. As far as he could see in all directions, the bay was deserted. All sorts of tales about the vicious creatures were being told. Some were likely true, and others were probably exaggerated to make a good story. Not only would a killer whale gladly gobble up anybody he happened to find in the water, some folks were saying, but he would also smash a small boat if he were hungry enough, just so he could get at the people in it. True or not, the story had effectively swept small boats off the bay.

Still, a cooling swim would sure be nice. . . .

He leaned and, scooping up a sand dollar, sailed it out over the water. It was not often that Bud Ricks willfully disobeyed his father, and this was not going to be one of those rare times.

He walked on, pausing from time to time to examine something cast ashore by the tide. He had almost reached the camp area when something caught his eye. It lay partially under some seaweed at the high-water mark where the last high tide must have deposited it. A puzzled look on his face, Bud dropped down on one knee and pushed the seaweed back. Beneath it was a black skin-diving fin. He picked it up curiously and, turning it this way and that, wondered how it happened to be here. Judging from the adjustment of the heel strap it must have been worn by someone with a large foot. Suddenly it flashed through his mind that it might have belonged to Jack Finch!

"Come on, Flipper!" Bud yelled excitedly. "We've got to get back and show this to Dad!"

The pickup truck was just pulling in beside the house when Bud came dashing up the path from the beach. Out of breath, the boy slid to a halt as Porter Ricks climbed out of the cab.

"Hey, what's the rush all about, Son?" Porter said.

"This . . ." Bud gasped, trying to catch his breath. He held out the flipper. "I—found this—washed up on the beach—down at the point."

His father took it and looked it over curiously. He lifted his gaze after a moment and stared out at the anchored schooner. "I wonder. . . ."

"Just what I was thinking, Dad!" exclaimed Bud. "Maybe it was Jack Finch's!"

"That's pretty straight thinking, Son. It seems to be a professional model, and the strap is adjusted for a good-sized foot. Finch was a pretty big fellow. You say you found it down at the point?"

Bud nodded excitedly. "Not far from the camp area!"

A skeptical look crossed Porter's face. "I don't know. That's a long way from where the dinghy was found the day he disappeared."

"Maybe the tide brought it up here."

"Could be."

"Why don't we take it out and show it to Dr. Avery and Mr. Latham? They ought to know if it was Jack Finch's or not."

Porter grinned down at his son and tousled his hair. "You're a regular detective today, Bud! Come on. We'll do just that."

Dr. Avery, as usual, was beneath the cockpit awning of the schooner with a book in his hands when the park launch drew alongside the larger vessel a

few minutes later. Whatever it was he was reading, it commanded his entire attention, for he did not notice he had visitors until Porter called out to him.

"Dr. Avery! We don't like to bother you, but Bud found something and we wanted you to have a look at it."

"Eh?" He looked up from his book. "What—oh! Here, let me take your bowline."

He laid the book aside and hurried to the rail. Bud tossed him a line and the launch was eased in against the canvas fenders hanging off the port side of the schooner. Bud and Porter climbed aboard the "Shark" and gave the rubber fin to the professor.

"Do you recognize it?" Porter asked. "We thought it might possibly have been Finch's."

A strange expression flickered across Dr. Avery's face as he took the fin. "I—I don't know. It's the same brand of equipment that we use. However, it would be impossible to make a positive identification."

"But it is the same brand?"

The professor nodded. Just then, the scowling face of Mel Latham appeared at the companionway hatch.

"What's that?" he said.

The professor held it out to him and repeated what

Porter had said about its being found on the beach.

"It was right over there," Bud put in, pointing toward the beach at the mouth of the lagoon.

"It ain't Jack's," Latham said abruptly and pushed it back toward Porter. "How could it be? It was miles from here where the killer got him."

"It's been more than a week," Porter said. "The tide could have brought it this far."

"Of course," the professor said, "it *is* a possibility, Mel."

The big man's brow darkened. "Here, let me see it again." He took the fin and examined it with great care. "Maybe so. Yeah . . . it could be poor Jack's."

Porter watched the two men carefully. There was something very odd about their behavior. The professor seemed nervous, and Mel Latham was almost belligerent. "Well," he said. "I'll take it into town to the coroner's office."

"What does the coroner want with it?" demanded Latham. "It's good as new. We might as well put it back with the other diving equipment."

"It's the only thing of Finch's that's turned up so far," Porter said. "If the coroner's office says it's okay, I'll bring it back to you."

Porter and Bud got into the launch and headed across the lagoon to the dock. As they tied up the boat Bud looked out at the "Shark" and frowned. "They acted kind of . . . I don't know . . . kind of funny, Dad. I mean, like they didn't want us to find Mr. Finch's fin."

"They did act strange, Son." He put his arm around Bud's shoulder as they walked up to the house. "Don't let it bother you. They're still probably pretty well shaken up about what happened to their friend."

Bud looked up into his father's face. He could see that Porter Ricks wasn't satisfied with his own explanation. The boy jammed one hand into his pocket, and, feeling the cold biscuit there, he suddenly remembered that he hadn't gotten down to the camp area and that hoped-for piece of Mrs. Aldridge's chocolate cake yet. "I forgot something, Dad. See you later!" And he turned and ran down to the beach.

6. Storm Coming

The telephone at the Rickses' house rang at a few minutes past nine, just as Porter informed Bud for the second time that he was to take his bath and get ready to turn in.

"I'll get it, Dad," Bud said cheerily, glad for the interruption.

"*I'll* get it," his father retorted, aiming one finger meaningfully toward the bathroom. He went into his office and scooped up the phone. "Coral Key Park. Ranger Ricks speaking."

"Porter," said the voice on the other end of the line, "Ed Bentley here. There's been a change in the weather advisory on that storm. I thought I'd better give you a call just in case you weren't listening to the radio."

"What is it, Ed?" he asked the Coast Guard officer.

"Well, the thing has done a complete about-face. Instead of heading away from our area, the devilish thing is aimed right down our throat. The weather bureau says the winds are still about fifty knots maximum, with plenty of lightning and rain. I thought you'd want to batten things down out there."

"Right, Ed. I've got some visitors in the park, and I'd better let them know about this, too."

"The 'Shark'?"

"That's right. And some campers, as well. Thanks for calling."

"That's okay. Glad to do it. If anything new develops we'll get in touch. Good night."

"What was that all about, Dad?" Sandy asked, looking up from Dr. Avery's book, which he had been reading.

Bud, still fully clothed and hoping for a last-minute reprieve, stuck his head in the door. He had a towel slung over one shoulder to indicate to his father that the last order had not been completely ignored.

"That storm that's been churning around out at sea for the past couple of days. It looks like it's made up its mind to tackle Coral Key after all. Come on in, Bud. Looks like you'll have to put off taking that bath for a while, much as you hate to do that."

"Gee, Dad," he said, shaking his head but having difficulty hiding a grin.

Porter said, "I'm going to drive over to the south camp area and notify the Aldridges and some new people who came in this afternoon. You two hop in the skiff and run out to the 'Shark.' According to Lieutenant Bentley, if the storm keeps on this present course it should hit here just before daybreak. Tell Dr. Avery to keep his radio tuned to the Coast Guard frequency. They'll be broadcasting any changes."

"Dad," Sandy said, scratching his cheek, "wouldn't you rather I went down to the camp area?"

Porter Ricks grinned at his older son. "I'll tell the young lady to get buttoned up for the big blow. You two just do as your old man says."

"Come on, lover boy," Bud teased.

"Oh, pipe down, shrimp!" Sandy took a swipe at his brother, but Bud agilely dodged out of reach and out the door and down toward the dock.

By the time Sandy got there, Bud was already in the skiff. "Did you put any gasoline in this today?" he asked.

"No. I thought you were going to do that. Is it empty?"

Bud nodded. "Almost. How about your running up to the shed and getting some?"

"Why me? *You* go get it. Oh, never mind." Sandy jumped down into the skiff. "It's not so far out there, and I don't mind rowing." He took up the oars and fitted them into the oarlocks, and when Bud had let the dock lines loose, Sandy leaned into the oars and headed across the lagoon.

The night was calm. The only sign of the approaching storm was the overcast that blotted out the moon and stars. Sandy aimed the boat for the white anchor light of the schooner.

There was no sound on the calm water except for the constant purr of the generator aboard the "Shark." As they drew closer to the vessel, Sandy paused and leaned on his oars. "See anybody on deck, Bud?" he asked.

"Nope. But there's a couple of portholes with a light showing. I guess one of 'em is the professor's cabin. He's probably reading. He must have read a million books. Every time you see him he's reading something."

"I guess being a professor, you have to read a lot."

"Yeah. It's a wonder his eyes don't get sore or something."

Sandy grinned and dipped the oars again into the water. Then he paused and cocked his head. "Say . . . do you hear somebody talking?"

The skiff had drifted to within fifty feet of the schooner. Bud listened intently for several moments, then nodded. "Yeah. Sounds like the professor to me. Come on. Let's get on over there."

Sandy resumed rowing and presently they drifted alongside the "Shark." "Bud, wait," Sandy said. "Those voices. . . ."

"Sounds like the professor and Latham. Who else could it be?"

"I thought I heard another voice. It sounded kind of familiar."

"You know, I was thinking the same thing. But —but there's not anybody else out here."

The two boys sat quietly for several moments. There was definitely a buzz of voices somewhere aboard the schooner. "There *are* other voices, Bud—" Sandy whispered. But he got no further, for suddenly a blaze of light flashed on in the mast spreaders overhead, almost blinding them in its brilliance. There was the sound of hurried footsteps somewhere on the deck of the schooner, and then a harsh and angry voice.

"Hey! What are you doing sneaking around out here?"

It was Mel Latham. As their eyes became accustomed to the light, they could see him standing right there above them on the deck, his dark eyes glaring down at them.

"What are you doing out here this time of night?" he boomed. "You come prying around here and you'll find trouble!"

"We weren't prying or sneaking, sir," Sandy said. "We just came out to—"

"Weren't prying, huh? All right, how come you were rowing instead of running your motor? Answer me that!"

"The—the motor was out of gas," Bud put in. "Honest, Mr. Latham, we didn't mean to—"

"Out of gas, is it? Well, we'll just have a look and see if you're lying. Lay alongside here. Come on!"

"What's the difficulty, Mel?" It was Dr. Avery who appeared beside the big fellow at the schooner's rail. "Well, good evening, Sandy, Bud."

"Caught these kids nosing around," Latham said.

"That's not right, Dr. Avery!" Sandy protested hotly. "Dad sent us out to tell you about the change in the weather report. Lieutenant Bentley called Dad and said the storm that's out at sea now has reversed course and is headed this way. It's due to hit Coral Key sometime before dawn tomorrow."

Mel Latham swung over the rail and dropped agilely into the skiff. "We'll see about that 'out of gas' business." He unscrewed the cap from the gas tank, then picked up the can and shook it. "Well . . . I guess you were telling the truth about that. Still, it ain't healthy to come poking around at night."

"It's not important, Mel," said the professor. "We appreciate your going to the trouble of coming out here to tell us. Thank you."

"It wasn't any trouble, sir," Sandy said. "Oh, I almost forgot. Dad said that if you wanted to keep posted to tune in the Coast Guard frequency on your radio."

"Good. We'll do that."

Mel Latham swung back aboard the schooner and gave the skiff a shove. As Sandy slipped the oars back into the oarlocks and prepared to head back, there was a loud crash below deck aboard the "Shark." The two boys looked back in surprise. The professor and Latham were still standing at the rail, and now the two men were staring hard at each other.

"What—what was that?" said Bud.

It was Latham who answered. "It—it wasn't nothing. A bottle in the galley probably. Must have rolled off. Now clear out of here."

Sandy dug his oars into the water and the skiff moved silently away. The boys didn't speak until they were absolutely certain they were out of earshot of the men aboard the schooner. Then Bud whispered, "There's something funny going on out there. I think there's somebody else on the 'Shark.' "

"Why would something just—just roll off the counter in the galley? The boat sure wasn't rocking. The lagoon is as calm as it ever gets."

"And what about those voices?" said Bud. "And Latham, he was sure fit to be tied when he first saw us. I don't mind telling you, I was mighty glad to see the professor."

Sandy rested on the oars for a moment and gazed back at the schooner. The floodlights in the mast spreaders had been turned off, but the portholes were still lighted. "Bud, how *could* anybody else be out there? We would have seen him by now, wouldn't we?"

"Yeah, I suppose we would have. Anyhow, why would anybody be hiding out there?"

As he rowed on toward the dock, Sandy said, "Let's see what Dad thinks about it. Maybe he can figure it out."

Porter Ricks returned to the house a few minutes after the boys got there. They told him of the voices they had heard, and of something crashing below while both the professor and Mel Latham were on deck. Porter mulled it over for a moment and then shook his head. "Maybe it was a radio you heard. Or perhaps it was simply Latham and Dr. Avery talking."

"All right," Bud said, "what about that crash we heard?"

Porter shrugged. "Something could have rolled off and crashed. It would take only a very slight movement of the boat for something like a glass or a bottle to roll off a counter."

The boys looked at each other. It could have happened that way. Still, they weren't at all convinced of it. The trouble was, how else could it be explained?

"Come on, boys," Porter said. "Let's forget about that and check the lines on the launch and the skiff. Then we'd better get some sleep. If the storm hits us, we're liable to have a pretty busy day tomorrow."

"But, Dad," Bud said, unwilling to give up, "can't we do something?"

"Do what, Son? I've got no business nosing around the schooner. Besides, suppose there was someone else on board? They're still not breaking any of the park regulations."

But even as he said it, Porter felt the same skepticism that the boys felt. There was definitely something strange about the "Shark" and her crew, and he was beginning to wish he had not given them permission to set up housekeeping in the lagoon.

The storm struck Coral Key with sudden fury a half an hour before dawn. Bud was abruptly awakened from a sound sleep by a violent crash of thunder that seemed to come from directly above the house. He crawled out of his bed and walked through the darkened house to the front porch. All around, blasts of wind slashed through the palm trees. Rain came down in great sheets, drenching everything. There was a brilliant flash of lightning, and Bud clearly saw the sleek hull of the schooner across the whitecaps of the lagoon. The wind whipped at the canopy over the vessel's cockpit, and in the brief illumination Bud thought he saw the form of a man on deck near the mainmast.

Another bolt of lightning zigzagged through the angry sky, lighting the lagoon as bright as midday. The "Shark" seemed almost alive, tugging fiercely at her anchor line with her bow into the wind. If the anchor line were to let go, Bud thought, it would only be a matter of minutes before the schooner piled up on the beach across the lagoon. Then he saw the man on deck. He had moved forward and was checking the anchor, his shoulders hunched against

the driving wind and rain. Probably Mel Latham.

"Really some storm, huh?"

Startled, Bud whirled around to see his father standing behind him. "Gee, Dad, you scared me. Yeah, it's a real dilly of a storm, all right. I sure hope they had sense enough to double-check their anchor out there before now."

"Not much doubt on that score, I would think. Latham strikes me as being a pretty fair seaman, and the professor's no slouch himself."

Sandy came out and stood with them. They watched for a while as the lightning and thunder continued. The surface of the lagoon was whipped to a white froth by the intensity of the wind.

"I wonder where Flipper goes during a storm," Bud said.

Porter laughed and put his hand on the boy's shoulder. "Don't you worry about Flipper. Dolphins have been looking after themselves for millions of years. I'm sure he knows just what to do."

"I'm not so sure after listening to the professor tell about that killer whale with thirteen dolphins in his stomach."

"Do the boats look okay?" Sandy asked. Another flash of lightning lit up the lagoon. The two boats could be seen pitching up and down in the waves at the dock, but plenty of fenders had been rigged alongside each of them, and if the storm did not last too long, there was little chance that either boat would be damaged.

"They look fine to me," Porter said. He glanced at his watch. "Well, it's almost five o'clock. We're going to have to do a lot of checking around the park when this blows over, so what do you fellas say we cook up some breakfast now?"

"Yeah!" agreed Bud, rubbing his hands together enthusiastically. "Let's eat!"

"Talk about a bottomless pit," Sandy said with a shake of his head. "Honest, Bud, I don't see how you can eat so much and not swell up like a balloon!"

Bud ignored the remark. "What about wheat cakes, sausage, fried eggs, and biscuits, Dad? Oh, yeah, and I'll slice up some of those potatoes we had last night and fry them!"

"Oh, brother!" wailed Sandy. Porter's laughter was drowned in a deep rumble of thunder as the three of them moved back into the house and began to prepare for the coming day.

7. Where Is Flipper?

The storm had abated almost entirely by nine o'clock that morning. The buffeting winds had died away, leaving only the faintest breeze. A thin, gray drizzle was all that remained of the driving rains, and where there had been raging whitecaps on the lagoon only hours before, there was now calm water marked by only the ground swell that came in from the open bay.

Porter Ricks and his two sons stood at the edge of the porch and looked out. "Well," Porter said, "I guess it's blown itself out. It was pretty wild while it lasted, though." He went back into the house and gathered up some papers from his desk. "The parks commissioner is due in on the nine-thirty train from the state capital. I'm to meet him and we're going

98

to the Coast Guard station and go over this killer whale business with Ed Bentley. How about you boys checking the boats first thing? They look all right from up here, but the lines may have chafed or loosened."

"Sure, Dad," Sandy said. "Want us to check around the park after we see to the boats? We wouldn't want the commissioner to come out here and find things in a mess, would we?"

Porter grinned and nodded. "Good thinking, Sandy. Check around, and I'll be back later."

When their father had climbed into the park truck and headed toward town, the boys walked down toward the dock. They saw at once that the storm had done more damage than they had first thought. Across the lagoon, on the shore beyond the schooner, lightning had struck a tall pine tree and split it down the trunk. The grounds all about the house and the dock were littered with broken branches and palm fronds. But the black schooner still lay serenely at anchor, as if there had been no storm at all.

"I don't reckon a storm like that is more than a good stiff breeze to an oceangoing schooner like the 'Shark,' " said Bud. "Look, there's Latham on deck now."

The big fellow, barefoot and wearing dungarees

and a T-shirt, walked about the decks, checking the halyards and other lines. He tightened the guy ropes of the cockpit awning which had worked loose in the wind. Then, seemingly satisfied that everything was shipshape, he went aft and vanished down the companionway hatch. Already a little spiral of smoke was drifting up into the misty morning air from the Charley Noble above the galley, indicating that the two men were preparing breakfast.

A check of the skiff and the launch showed that both boats had weathered the storm. The constant pitching and bobbing in the high winds had caused one of the dock lines to wear dangerously thin, and Sandy spliced a new one to replace it.

"Bud, how about your picking up this mess around here?" Sandy asked. "I'd like to go down to the camp area and see if the folks down there might need any help."

Bud started to ride his brother about his new girl friend, Sally Aldridge, but he was not in the mood for teasing. "Sure, Sandy, you go ahead. And if Mrs. Aldridge has got any of that chocolate cake left, see if you can wrangle me a slice. A big one, with plenty of icing."

"Fair enough!" Sandy answered, pleasantly surprised by his kid brother's unexpected attitude. The park jeep was in the shed behind the house. He cranked it up and, with a wave to Bud, went bouncing away down the trail toward the camping grounds.

Bud soon realized there was more work than he thought to gathering up the litter left by the storm, and nearly an hour had passed by the time the area surrounding the house and the dock was in spick-and-span shape. Satisfied with the job, he rewarded himself with a peanut-butter-and-jelly sandwich and a tall glass of ice-cold milk. Then he strolled down to the lagoon and, sticking the old Klaxon into the water, gave the horn a firm squeeze.

"Flipper!" he called. "Hey, Flipper! Come on, boy!"

He gave the horn another squeeze. *Honk! Honk!* it went beneath the water. But nothing happened. There was no sign of life in the lagoon. The "Shark" rode smoothly at anchor. The surface of the water was calm except for a gentle swell that rolled in from the bay as the aftermath of the storm.

A frown creased Bud's freckled features. A vague feeling of worry began to grow inside him. Had something happened to Flipper? He usually came streaking to the dock when the horn was blown. But there were times when Flipper was too far away to hear the honking. Maybe he was off someplace catching his breakfast, or just visiting with other dolphins in the bay.

Bud decided to wait awhile and try again. He went back up to the house and turned on the radio while he cleaned up his bedroom. A newscast came on, and he sat down at his desk to listen. The announcer said that the state commissioner of parks had arrived and was at this very minute touring the area where the killer whale attack was presumed to have taken place. Ranger Porter Ricks and Lt. Ed Bentley were with the high official.

Bud had been trying very hard to put the killer whale out of his thoughts, but now he found it impossible. He hurried back down to the lagoon and tried again to summon Flipper with the horn. But, as before, the dolphin failed to respond. This time Bud could not rid himself of the feeling that something terrible had happened to Flipper. All the terrible stories he had heard about killer whales came flooding into his brain—especially the story about the thirteen dolphins that were found in the stomach of a killer whale.

His face suddenly brightened, and he snapped his fingers. There *was* a place he could go look for Flipper. "The secret cove!" he exclaimed. Flipper had probably been hungry when the storm ended, and he might have gone there looking for food.

The cove, which was half a mile up the bay, was not really a secret. Bud and Sandy had named it that when they discovered that they could often find Flipper there when he was nowhere else to be found. It was a very good place for rounding up mullet and schools of other fish, and Flipper and other dolphins often went there to catch their dinners.

Without really thinking, Bud rushed up to the shed and brought a five-gallon can of outboard fuel down to the dock. He poured it into the empty tank in the skiff, then hastily cast off the lines and cranked the engine. The boat circled smoothly and gathered speed across the lagoon, throwing white sheets of spray out from the bows.

As he neared the "Shark," he throttled back. Maybe Dr. Avery or Mel Latham had seen Flipper during the morning. But neither man was on deck, and Bud decided against the delay and twisted the throttle again to the high speed position. As he passed astern of the big schooner, he glanced over and thought he saw a face at the companionway.

The skiff shot out of the lagoon, and Bud turned northward, cruising along twenty or thirty yards out from the beach. The drizzle had stopped altogether, and the clouds were beginning to break up.

Here and there patches of clean blue sky showed through.

After a five-minute ride he spotted the narrow entrance to the cove. He slowed the boat and eased into the cove. On all sides the shore was covered with dense thickets of mangrove. Many small birds flew about in the tangled branches, and on the opposite side of the cove a long-legged white heron tiptoed through the shallow water, searching for an unwary fish on which to dine.

Bud shut the motor off and picked up the Klaxon horn. But before he had a chance to sound it, he saw a swirl in the water nearby, and suddenly Flipper's grinning face appeared beside the skiff. The dolphin tossed his head and squawked a greeting to his friend.

"So this is where you were all the time!" Bud exclaimed. "And I was worried about you! Come on, let's go back to Coral Key. Haven't you heard? It's dangerous wandering around in the bay these days."

Flipper replied by jabbering away in rapid-fire fashion. Then he ducked under the water, got a good start, and came flying through the air right across the boat.

"You crazy nut!" Bud yelled gleefully. He was greatly tempted to pull off his shirt and dive in. There

was a diving mask in the boat, and he could hold onto Flipper's dorsal fin and have a fine underwater ride.

But he put the temptation aside. Instead, he cranked up the motor and called to Flipper, "Come on! Let's go!"

Flipper, however, had other plans. He lifted his head up and gave it a shake. Near the shore of the cove Bud saw two other dolphins break the surface for a breath, and he realized they were working together rounding up food.

"So you haven't had breakfast yet, huh?" Bud said to Flipper. "Okay. But come on home when you're finished."

Flipper streaked off to join his companions, and Bud, satisfied that his pet was safe and sound—at least for the time being—opened the throttle and headed back for the lagoon. The sky had cleared almost completely, and the warm sun shone down brightly.

It was going to be an ideal day for swimming or fishing or a little skin diving. As the boat skimmed across the bay, Bud gazed out toward the chain of small islands that marked the outer edge of Coral Key Marine Preserve. Suddenly an idea occurred to him. There might be a way he could cool off and still not really disobey his father's instructions against going into the bay. There were several tidal pools out there beyond Rock Island. Almost every time he had been there Bud had been able to catch a few lobsters, and lobster was one of his favorite dishes, and also a favorite of Sandy's and their father's. The pools were outside the boundaries of the preserve, so there was no regulation against catching lobsters. And the water across the reefs that formed the pools was so shallow that a killer whale could not possibly get into them. The pools were 100 percent safe— Bud knew that. He could swim and dive without fear.

Of course, Bud told himself, his father had actually said keep out of the water. But the only reason he said it was because of the killer whale, and if the place was 100 percent safe. . . .

His face broke into a big grin as he reached his decision. He turned the boat, took aim toward the north end of little Rock Island, and struck out across the broad expanse of the bay. A few nicely broiled lobster tails with a little lemon juice and melted butter over them would go a long way toward making Porter Ricks realize his younger son had not really gone against his orders.

The decision was one that Bud was going to regret.

8. A Killer Whale

Rock Island, one of a number of small islands that lay strung out along the eastern edge of Coral Key Marine Preserve, was scarcely two hundred yards in length and certainly not more than one hundred yards in width. It was low-lying, crowned with a dense growth of coconut palms, and surrounded by coral reefs. Actually, the island itself was built up from the coral reefs surrounding it and had been misnamed Rock Island by some traveler long forgotten who had first set foot there and marked it on a chart. Beneath the island, as was the case with the others, numerous small and large caves and grottoes had been created by the combined action of time and tide. On the eastern shore of the island there were large tidal pools.

Bud carefully skirted the dangerous coral heads that existed just beneath the surface as he circled the island. He aimed for a small, crescent-shaped white beach and expertly nosed the skiff ashore. He climbed out and tossed the anchor up on the sand, then got his diving mask and swim fins from the boat and put them on. Lastly, he took a gunnysack from beneath the forward seat, and, grinning happily, he said, "Watch out, lobsters! Here comes the great Bud Ricks!"

He stalked out into the pool several yards farther along the beach, and when the depth of the water reached his chest, he took a breath and went under. The bottom of the tidal pool shelved away ahead of him to a depth of ten or twelve feet. Coral formations created a fantasy land as he drifted weightless above them. Sea fans waved gracefully in the slight current, and brightly colored tropical fish of many kinds paused in their constant battle for survival to see what strange creature had come to visit them.

As he moved along slowly, kicking his fins rhythmically, he spotted the long, wirelike feelers of several lobsters waving out of holes in the coral. He gave a strong kick and angled for the bottom, where he grabbed the first feelers he came to, hauled the jerking lobster from its hiding place, and stuck it into the sack. Unlike the northern variety, these creatures had no large claws, and they were helpless against him except for their ability to move fast and hide in cracks and crevices.

After bagging two nice ones, Bud shot to the surface for air. Then he darted down for two more. He was having great fun after having been grounded for so many days. When he had captured six, he swam back to the shallow water and waded up onto the beach. He dumped his catch into the boat and examined them critically.

"I guess you fellows are big enough," he said, pleased with himself. "Two for Dad, two for Sandy, and two for me. No need to be greedy!"

He tossed the fins and mask beneath the seat and pushed the boat off the beach. As he started the outboard, he was already trying to think of the best explanation to give his father for going into the water when he had been told not to. He threaded the skiff through the coral heads and, with Rock Island astern, gave the motor full throttle and set his course for the distant shore of Coral Key.

He had gone only a couple of hundred yards when something very unusual caught his attention. There was something strange about the water dead ahead

of the boat, and he slowed and peered toward it. As
the boat drifted toward the spot, he saw that it was a
stream of bubbles coming to the surface. He shut
off the motor and scratched his head. How could
this be? The water on this side of the islands and
reefs was about fifty or sixty feet deep. He gazed
intently down into the greenish depths. It was very
puzzling. The only thing Bud could think of that
would produce such bubbles would be a diver using
an aqualung.

But that was hardly possible, not after the warnings that the Coast Guard had issued to divers and
others to stay out of the bay. Not only that. Even if
the bay were as safe as a bathtub, why would anyone be diving in this particular spot? There was
nothing here of interest to divers.

The bubbles continued to fizz up and pop at the
surface. There was *something* down there, of that
Bud was certain. But what? He stood up in the boat
and, shielding his eyes against the glare, looked
around in all directions. There was not another boat
in sight. The only sign of life he saw was the oc-
casional splash of a fish or a wandering gull in the
sky.

He would have to report this, and so he gauged
the distance and direction from Rock Island as best

he could. "Looks like about two hundred yards," he mused. "And it's just about due west of the north tip of the island. Gee, I wish Flipper were here to go down and have a look. Maybe. . . ." He was thinking, even as he gripped the cord to restart the engine, that it would take only a minute or two to don his mask and fins, slip over the side, and scoot down deep enough to see what was producing the bubbles.

Still, Porter Ricks had told both his sons in no uncertain terms that they were to keep out of the bay. Undecided, Bud watched in fascination as the bubbles continued to boil up all about the boat. If they were being made by an aqualung, there would have to be more than one to be sending up so much air.

His curiosity was too strong to overcome, and, hurriedly putting on the mask and fins so that he would not have time to reconsider, he took a couple of deep breaths and slipped over the gunwale of the skiff into the water. He took a length of line, one end of which was tied to a cleat, so that if a breeze sprung up the boat would not drift away.

The water closed over his head, and he found himself in the midst of the rising air bubbles rushing up from the depths. He swam slowly downward, feeling the pressure of the water increasing against his ears. The water was not as clear as he had thought. The storm had stirred up the bay, and when he got down to a depth of fifteen feet all he could make out below were the shadowy outlines of several huge outcroppings of brain coral. The source of the bubbles was in the murky depths below that.

He swam down as far as the line from the boat would allow. He needed a breath, and he also began to feel uneasy about being in the water alone. One of the most important rules of diving was for the diver never to go in alone, and this seemed especially important now.

He turned and began to kick for the surface. His mind was made up now. He had acted foolishly. He would get back in the boat and get to Coral Key as fast as he could. His father, and maybe Lieutenant Bentley, would want to know about these mysterious bubbles.

His head broke the surface, and he pushed the mask back onto his forehead. The boat was twenty feet off to his right, so he turned loose the line and began to swim. Suddenly his eyes became round as saucers. He stopped and, treading water, stared just behind the boat. There was something dark beneath the water, something large. It seemed only a shadow at first, but he realized there was nothing there to cast a shadow. His heart pounded in his throat. The thing grew larger and more distinct as it came toward the surface. There was a rippling of the surface a few yards behind the outboard motor, and then something black and gleaming rose up into the air. It came up, up, rising four feet or more out of the water as it moved steadily toward the boy.

There was no mistaking what it was. He had seen pictures, and he had heard stories. Bud gave a strangled yell of terror. The huge triangular fin was now between him and the doubtful safety of the boat. In his panic he gulped water into his mouth. Choking, his arms and legs thrashing wildly in an effort to swim around the monster, Bud knew there was no chance of escape, and certainly no chance of help. Even if Flipper were there, he would be helpless against this terrible creature.

The huge fin seemed to be looming over him as something clamped tightly and painfully on his left ankle. His last memory was of being snatched violently beneath the water.

A few minutes later, a breeze ruffled the bay, and the skiff, with its line trailing overboard and a cargo of six lobsters, began to drift slowly away toward the mainland. Not many yards away, a stream of bubbles continued to rise from the murky depths.

9. Searching

It was almost two o'clock when Porter Ricks got back to Coral Key after his meeting with the parks commissioner. Sandy had been back at the house for fifteen or twenty minutes and was eating a sandwich when his father came in.

"Where's Bud?" Porter said.

"Bud? I don't know. I just got back myself."

Porter walked out onto the porch, then turned and came quickly back in. "The skiff's gone. Did he say anything to you about using it?"

Sandy put his sandwich down on the plate. "No, sir. Maybe he went out to the 'Shark' in it."

"There's nothing but the dinghy out there. Have you got any other idea where he might have gone?"

Sandy thought for a moment. "Well, you know

how worried he's been about Flipper lately. There's a little cove up the bay where we can usually find Flipper when he's not around here. We could check with Dr. Avery and Mr. Latham. Maybe they noticed which way he went."

Porter walked outside again, a look of deep concern on his face. Across the lagoon the black schooner swung easily on her anchor line. Beneath the cockpit awning, Dr. Avery sat in the shade with his pipe in his mouth and a book in his hands. For a man going on a Central American expedition, Porter thought to himself, he still seemed strangely unoccupied. He acted more as if he were merely waiting for something to happen.

"All right, Sandy, you go down and start the engines on the launch. I'll get my binoculars and join you."

Sandy had both motors purring smoothly when Porter jumped aboard. They crossed the lagoon to the "Shark." The professor watched them approach, and when they drew alongside he laid his book aside and came to the rail.

"Good afternoon, Mr. Ricks, Sandy. Anything wrong? You look worried."

"We're trying to find Bud, Dr. Avery," Porter said. "We believe he's gone off in the skiff, and under the present conditions I'd just as soon not have him wandering about the bay alone. He may have gone someplace looking for Flipper. Did you happen to see the skiff leave the lagoon?"

The professor shook his head. "No, I didn't. However, Mel's below. Maybe he saw him."

Porter held onto the rail stanchions while the professor disappeared down the companionway. Moments later the swarthy face of Mel Latham appeared.

"What do you want, Ranger?" the big fellow said. "I'm busy." He stepped on deck and sat down atop the cabin, smoothing the ends of his bushy moustache.

Dr. Avery followed him up. "Have you seen the younger Ricks boy, Mel?"

"What do you mean, have I seen him? I ain't got time to go watching after some kid!"

"We're not expecting you to watch after him, Mr. Latham," Porter said, trying to keep from losing his temper. "He went out in the skiff while Sandy and I were away. We're trying to get a lead on which way he went so we can find him."

Latham squinted thoughtfully. "Lemme think. Yeah, I believe I did get a glimpse of him when he came past here."

"What time was it? And which direction did he go when he reached the bay?"

Latham brushed again at his moustache, as if in doubt. "Wasn't paying much attention, but it seems like it might have been around ten, eleven o'clock. Maybe even a little bit later. He turned north soon as he cleared the lagoon."

"He may have been heading for the cove, Dad," said Sandy. "But that isn't more than a five-minute run from here."

Porter rubbed his chin slowly. "Maybe he ran out of gas."

"I doubt that," said Sandy with a shake of his head. "It was empty last night, and he would have had to gas it up before he left. He probably took one of the five-gallon cans of fuel." He glanced briefly at Mel Latham's dark face, recalling the unfriendly reception he and Bud had gotten the previous night when they rowed out to the schooner.

Dr. Avery also shot a quick glance at the big man, then looked back to Porter Ricks and smiled weakly. "Well, boys will be boys. They can be very forgetful when they're off somewhere having fun. They don't realize just how concerned we adults become."

Porter nodded skeptically. "I hope that's all it is.

Thanks for your help. Oh, Dr. Avery . . . if he happens to come back before we do, tell him to get right up to the house and call us on the shortwave radio, will you?"

"I'll do better than that," said the professor. "I'll call you at once on our radio. I—I know what it means to be worried about a son."

Mel Latham gave the professor a strange look, then ambled down the companionway. Porter eased away from the schooner and pushed both throttles full ahead. The powerful engines shot the sleek boat forward in a shower of white spray, and they turned north.

Minutes later they idled into the cove. A half a dozen dolphins were working back and forth along the shore, and every few seconds there was a great flurry of activity and much splashing about.

"Looks like they've rounded up a school of mullet and are feeding," Porter said. "Do you see Flipper?"

Sandy picked up the binoculars and peered through them. "I can't tell, they're making such a splash. Wait—yeah! There's Flipper! He sees us!"

One of the dolphins had moved away from the others and had his head sticking up out of the water. He gazed toward the boat just as a human swimmer might have done. His sleek head bobbed up and down and he began to squawk and jabber, as though to tell his friends in the boat that he was busy now and would see them later. Then, with a graceful leap, he spun around and hurried back with his fellow dolphins.

"Well," Porter said, "we still don't know if Bud came up here or not. He's certainly not here now." His eyes scanned the entire shoreline of the cove. "I wonder where else he might have gone?"

"You don't suppose Mel Latham might have been wrong, do you, Dad?" said Sandy. "I mean about which way Bud went in the skiff?"

Porter turned the boat and moved slowly into the bay again. "I don't know, Son." He was about to give the motors full throttle when something caught his eye. He climbed over the windshield onto the forward deck and stood up. "Hand me the binoculars, Sandy." He shielded his eyes with one hand and squinted off toward the southeast. Sandy gave him the binoculars, and Porter quickly adjusted the focus.

"What do you see?" Sandy asked curiously.

"I'm not sure. Maybe it was just a pelican or— no! It's a boat out on the bay. You don't see many boats out these days. Let's run out there. Maybe they happened to see our skiff."

Porter climbed back over and took the controls.

The launch shot forward under full power and headed toward the distant speck on the sparkling waters of the bay. As they rode, Sandy picked up the binoculars and tried to focus on the object. This was difficult to do because of the bouncing of the launch, but as the distance grew shorter he was able to tell more about the boat ahead of them. His heart fell. "Dad . . . Dad, that looks like the skiff out there."

"Are you sure? Maybe the motor's just broken down. Bud wouldn't have stopped on purpose out there."

"I—I can't see Bud in the boat. It looks like it's— it's empty."

"What? Here, you take the wheel." Porter Ricks grabbed the binoculars and, putting his feet apart to steady himself, put the glasses to his eyes. The little boat seemed to spring at him as it came into sharp focus. There was no doubt, it was the skiff. And unless Bud was lying down on one of the seats, the boat was empty.

The launch sped on, closing the gap between it and the skiff. Diamonds of spray scattered from beneath as the craft roared onward. As they drew near, Sandy pulled back on the throttle and expertly maneuvered alongside the smaller boat.

Porter climbed over into the skiff. There were six lobsters scuttling about in the bottom. Bud's T-shirt lay crumpled on the stern seat. A line dangled overboard into the water. But there was no sign of the boy.

Sandy joined his father and made a quick search beneath the seats. "Dad, the diving mask and fins are missing. We always keep them in here. Bud must have—"

"Gone diving?" Porter supplied. "After I told him to stay out of the water?"

"I know it doesn't make any sense that he would have disobeyed you," Sandy said. "If he did, there must have been a good reason."

"You call these lobsters a good reason? I don't."

"Dad! That's probably it! You know those tidal pools on the other side of Rock Island? Well, they're outside the preserve and they're a good safe place to dive. There are always lobsters there. Maybe he's out there, and the boat just drifted away!"

Porter got the binoculars again and gazed toward Rock Island, which was approximately a mile to the east. He scanned the tiny island from one end to the other. If Bud was marooned, it stood to reason that he would be on the beach on this side, watching for someone to find the skiff. There was no sign at all of him. Porter lowered the binoculars slowly.

"Let's get over there, Sandy. I don't see him, but he might be on the other side of the island."

The skiff was tied astern of the launch, and they sped to the small island, where they beached both boats. Very soon, they found Bud's footprints in the sand on the small beach near the tidal pools.

"Look!" Sandy said. "The boat was beached here!"

They examined the marks. Porter straightened slowly after a while, his expression drawn and serious. "Bud's tracks show that he left the boat and also came back. I don't think the boat drifted away, Sandy. Bud took it away. Whatever happened to him, it was after he left here."

"But—but what could have happened to him?"

"I don't know. But let's search the whole island, and if there are no more signs of him, we'll call the Coast Guard."

The search was fruitless, and as they got back into the launch and shoved off, Sandy's face brightened momentarily. "We didn't check the motor in the skiff, Dad. Maybe it broke down and somebody picked Bud up and took him in."

Before his father could reply, Sandy climbed over into the smaller boat. For once he hoped that the engine would not start when he yanked on the cord.

But it did, and on the very first pull. Porter had known that it would, for anyone picking up Bud under such circumstances would certainly have towed in the skiff.

Porter picked up the microphone of the ship-to-shore radio. "Coast Guard Radio, this is W-D nine-five-nine-eight," he said in a flat voice. "Coast Guard Radio, this is W-D nine-five-nine-eight. Come in, please."

The speaker crackled briefly, and a voice said, "W-D nine-five-nine-eight, this is Coast Guard Radio, Coral Key Station. Over."

"This is Ranger Ricks. Is Lieutenant Ed Bentley there? Over."

There was a momentary silence, then a voice responded, "Porter? Ed Bentley here. Over."

"We're at Rock Island, Ed. We've found our outboard skiff adrift on the bay. Bud was using it, and he's—he's missing. We'd like your assistance with a search. Over."

"Any sign of what happened to him, Porter? Over."

"None." He stood with the microphone clenched in his fist. Somewhere out there on the peaceful, sunlit waters of the bay, something strange and terrible had happened to his son, just as something strange

and terrible had happened to Jack Finch. "We'll continue searching, Ed. Get out here as soon as you
can. W-D nine-five-nine-eight, out."

He slammed the microphone back on its hook and
started the engines.

10. Some Snapshots

If anything, the search for young Bud Ricks was even more intensive than that for Jack Finch. Porter Ricks and Sandy ran the launch until the fuel tanks were empty, and then they refueled and went out again. Flipper caught up to them during the afternoon and ranged ahead of the launch like a hunting dog from then on. The dolphin seemed to sense that something had happened, and even the playful grin that characterized his face seemed to have faded.

The search went on for two days, without any further clue as to Bud's fate. Though nothing official was said, it was being told all over the area that the killer whale had taken another victim. The same terrible thought had been on the minds of Bud's father and brother since the moment they found the skiff drifting empty on the bay.

As for Dr. Avery and Mel Latham, they offered their help in the futile search for the boy. In fact, almost everybody pitched in in one way or another. Dozens of small boats joined the search. Young Hank Peeler and his father kept their boat criss-crossing the bay from sunrise till long after dark. And Sally Aldridge and her parents, who had been tenting in the south camp area, helped by cleaning the Rickses' house and preparing their meals.

But after two days, most people held out little or no hope for the boy. As the launch pulled slowly into the dock late that afternoon, a sad-eyed Dr. Avery met them.

"I wish there were something I could do, Mr. Ricks," he said. "I have a son of my own, and I know how you must feel." He rubbed his small beard in an absentminded way. "All I can say is . . . is don't ever completely give up hope."

The professor's words stuck in Porter's mind. It was a strange thing to say, and he had the odd feeling that there was some hidden meaning behind them. It was almost as if the professor were trying to tell him that Bud was all right. Of course, that really made no sense, and Porter dismissed the thought.

Soon something happened at the Coast Guard station that was to take Porter Ricks's mind off Dr. Avery. The moment Lt. Ed Bentley got off the picket boat a yeoman handed him a slip of paper with a name on it, along with an envelope containing several photographs. The name on the paper was listed as George Holmes, and the photographs were interesting indeed.

"When did he bring these in?" Bentley asked the yeoman.

"About ten minutes ago. He says you can reach him at the Starlight Motel, where he and his family are staying."

Bentley went into his office and sat down at the desk. He reached Mr. George Holmes by telephone, talked with him for several minutes, then hung up. "Franklin!" he shouted to the yeoman. "Phone Ranger Ricks at Coral Key Park and tell him I'm on the way out there. Tell him I've got something I want him to take a look at."

"Yes, sir," Yeoman Franklin replied. He was picking up the phone as his commanding officer hurried out to the parking area and got into his car.

Not many minutes later, Lieutenant Bentley pulled to a stop at the Rickses' house. Porter and Sandy were at the door to meet him. The Coast-

guardsman wasted no time. He held out the envelope to Porter and said, "We've had quite a few verbal reports on the killer whale. We've been asking for more proof, and here it is."

The snapshots seemed to have been taken somewhere on the bay. And each of them clearly showed a black triangular fin sticking up from the water.

"Look, Dad!" Sandy said excitedly, putting his finger on one of the pictures. "You can see the South Reef light in the background on this one."

"That's right," Ed Bentley said. "Of course, we had no reason to think the pictures weren't authentic, but that makes it certain."

Porter nodded. It was indeed South Reef light, the metal framework built on the shoals to warn ships away. "Where did you get these, Ed? Who took them?"

"A tourist by the name of George Holmes brought them in. His daughter was standing on the point down there a few days ago taking pictures of a school of dolphins feeding near the shore. Take a close look there and you can see one or two of them in the foreground. She didn't know she had photographed this fin until the pictures were developed and they picked them up this afternoon."

Porter frowned, looking at each of the snapshots

again. "That's strange," he said.

"What do you mean?" asked the lieutenant.

"The dolphins feeding. Doesn't it strike you as odd that a school of dolphins, which are supposed to be one of the killer whale's favorite dishes, would be peacefully feeding with that fellow cruising around only a hundred yards or so from them?"

Bentley's brows rose and he rubbed his jaw. Then he gave his head a shake. "But there they are, right in the pictures. If that thing's not the dorsal fin of a killer whale, what the heck is it?"

Porter continued to examine the pictures. Then he said, "Let's show these to Dr. Avery. He knows quite a lot about them. Maybe he can explain it."

The sun had already set and dusk had settled over the lagoon as Porter, Sandy, and Lieutenant Bentley went down to the dock and headed across toward the schooner in the skiff.

Mel Latham was sitting atop the cabin, smoking a cigarette and drinking a cup of coffee as they pulled alongside. "We'd like to see Dr. Avery," Porter said.

"He's down in his cabin," Latham replied. "What is it you want?"

"We need his opinion on something. Will you hurry up and get him?"

"Not till I know what it is you want to bother him with," Latham said belligerently.

Porter glanced at Lieutenant Bentley, then grabbed a rail stanchion and swung himself up onto the schooner's deck. "I'll go down and get him myself."

Latham shot out a big hand and grabbed Porter's shirt. "Hold on there, mister! Don't nobody come busting aboard the 'Shark' telling Mel Latham what they're gonna do! Now you—"

At that moment, Dr. Avery appeared at the companionway hatch. "What's the trouble, Mel? Oh, it's you, Mr. Ricks."

Latham's hand dropped away slowly and Porter moved past him, carrying the envelope. "I'd like you to have a look at these snapshots, Dr. Avery. I'd like your opinion on the situation they seem to show."

"Situation? What situation?" He took the envelope and slipped the photos out. He moved to the open hatchway where light came up from the galley. He stared at each picture in turn, then went through them again before saying anything. "I . . . ah, I'd say this was the dorsal fin of an orca—a killer whale." He looked up from the pictures, a peculiar expression in his eyes. "Where were these taken?"

"Right out there in the bay," Lieutenant Bentley put in. "That's the South Reef light there in the background."

"Take another look, sir," Porter said. "Not at the background, but at the foreground. What is it you see?"

The scientist nodded. "A school of dolphins, apparently feeding."

"That's what puzzles us," Porter went on. "Would dolphins be peacefully feeding with perhaps their worst enemy that close by?"

Mel Latham had moved to the professor's side and had been looking at the snapshots. Before the professor could answer, Latham said, "Nothing strange about that. The killer just wasn't looking for food. They can tell about things like that. I've seen dolphins when killer whales were around, plenty of times."

Dr. Avery handed the pictures back to Porter. "Mel is right. As you know, dolphins, killer whales, and other cetaceans have a sort of sonar arrangement. They emit high frequency sounds and use the echo of these sounds in the same manner that man uses sonar and radar. Apparently, the orca in your photographs was sending out none of these sounds, and therefore the dolphins had no reason to be afraid."

"Well," Lieutenant Bentley said, "does that satisfy you, Porter? It sounds reasonable enough to me."

The professor frowned. "I don't quite understand, Mr. Ricks. If that was not the fin of an orca in those photographs, just what might it have been?"

Porter shook his head. "I'm not really sure what I was thinking. But there is something peculiar about what's been happening around here. For one thing, even though the killer whale undoubtedly prefers warm-blooded creatures in his diet, as far as I've been able to find out there is not a single positive case on record of a killer eating a human being."

"But you must admit there are many cases where the possibility exists," said the professor. "We certainly can't overlook that possibility here."

"I know," Porter said reluctantly. "Here, in the space of only a few days, we've got reason to believe there have been . . . been two victims."

"We'd better head back to shore," Lieutenant Bentley said quietly.

Porter and Sandy sat on the dock for some time after Lieutenant Bentley had driven back to the Coast Guard station. Night had fallen, and stars and a half-moon shone above.

"Dad," Sandy said after a while. "Dad, like the

professor said, if that isn't a killer whale, what could it be?"

Porter put one hand on the boy's shoulder. "I don't know, Son. But there's something about all this that just rubs me the wrong way."

"Me, too, Dad. But what is it?"

Just then there was a rush of water at the end of the dock, and Flipper's gleaming head poked up. He looked from Sandy to Porter, and then he looked all around the dock. After a few moments, he turned over on one side and gave a mournful whistling sound.

"Poor old Flipper misses Bud as much as we do," Sandy said. There were tears in his eyes as he turned and walked up toward the house.

11. Night Watch on the Lagoon

Sandy Ricks turned fitfully on his bed. Suddenly he sat upright, listening. Something had awakened him, but now all was quiet. Then he heard it again, and there was no mistaking that sound. It was the distinctive squawking and jabbering of Flipper.

Sandy leaped out of bed and rushed out to the porch. He had no idea of the time. It was after midnight, however, because the moon had already set. Down in the lagoon, Flipper set up a racket again, whistling and squeaking and splashing the water. Sandy's first thought was that the killer whale had come into the lagoon and that Flipper was in danger. But another sound changed his mind. It was Mel Latham's voice, carrying faintly across the water, but with definite tones of anger.

Sandy turned and ran back into the house and into his father's room. "Dad! Dad! Wake up!" He turned on the bedside light.

Porter sat up, blinking. "What is it, Son? What time is it?" He fumbled on the bedside table and picked up the alarm clock. The hands stood at fifteen minutes past one.

"There's something going on down in the lagoon, Dad. Flipper's raising all kinds of a ruckus down there, and Latham's hollering at him. Come on!"

Porter followed his son outside the house, where they stood in silence for several minutes. There was no sound at all from the lagoon. The night was so silent that it seemed to be pressing in on them.

"But Flipper *was* yakking away, Dad," Sandy said. "He woke me up."

"I'm sure he was, Son. I wonder what it was all about, though."

"He's always acted real funny about the 'Shark.' Of course, maybe he was just pestering Mr. Latham. He never has liked him since that first day."

"That might be," Porter replied. "But I wonder what Latham would be doing up this time of night. Sandy, go get the night binoculars out of my office. I want to take a look out there."

The boy disappeared into the house and returned

shortly with the glasses. They were special Navy-type binoculars with lenses designed to bring the clearest possible vision with a minimum of light.

Porter lifted the binoculars, adjusted the focus, and peered out at the schooner. It was still very difficult to see, even with the glasses. He scanned the dark decks, but there was no sign of activity. Suddenly, just ahead of the schooner, there was a big splash, and once more the familiar rapid-fire jabbering of Flipper sounded across the water.

"Did you see him?" Sandy whispered excitedly.

"I saw the splash, but I couldn't tell what it was all about. Maybe you're right. Flipper might be just pestering Latham. Still. . . ."

"Dad, you remember what Mr. Aldridge said about seeing something moving in toward the lagoon one night? You—you don't suppose Dr. Avery and Mr. Latham have got a—a *trained* killer whale, do you? I mean, the funny way Flipper acts, and Jack Finch and . . . and Bud disappearing the way they did."

Porter lowered the binoculars. "No, I don't think that. In the first place, what on earth would they do something like that for? It doesn't make sense. But there is something funny about the 'Shark.' "

"Something else bothers me, Dad. Do you think a

man like Dr. Avery would be involved in doing something that . . . well, that wasn't *right?* He's practically famous."

Porter took another look through the binoculars. The schooner lay peacefully at anchor. Nothing moved. It would be easier to observe from the opposite side of the lagoon, for the "Shark" was anchored much closer to that shore.

"We might as well get back to bed, Son," Porter said at last. "I want to be out on the bay at daybreak."

Flipper joined in the search the next morning with determination. He was fully aware that something had happened to his good friend Bud, and he was tireless in his efforts as he ranged far and wide ahead of Porter and Sandy, who followed in the park launch.

They crossed and recrossed the waters of the bay until nightfall, and when they returned to the lagoon, tired and hungry, Lieutenant Bentley was there to meet them.

"Porter," he said, "I know how this has hit you. The fact is, your two boys have been almost like sons to me. But holding out false hopes isn't going to do you or Sandy any good. You're just going to make it that much harder on yourselves to accept what's happened to Bud."

"Ed, I've got to have more proof than just an empty boat drifting on the bay."

Bentley sighed dispiritedly. "I hate to have to put it so bluntly, but if this killer whale *did* get the boy, there isn't going to be any more proof than we've already got. Not ever, Porter."

The muscles in Porter Ricks's jaw clenched and he gazed out at the bay. "I can't help but feel that Bud is alive. Don't ask me to explain it—I can't. It's just a—a feeling." He pointed out into the lagoon where a tired Flipper surfaced slowly for a breath. "He feels it, too. You should have seen him out there today, Ed. He never stopped."

"All right, Porter. If you won't give up, I won't, either. I'll have my men out again at the crack of dawn."

Later, after they had eaten dinner, Porter and Sandy sat in the quiet darkness on the front porch, neither finding much to say. The mast light of the "Shark" shone like a star across the lagoon. Light also showed from two portholes. Porter sat for a long time, sipping his after-dinner coffee and staring out at the schooner. Suddenly he gulped down the rest of the coffee and stood up.

"Sandy, I'm going to keep a watch on that boat tonight. I'm going to watch it all night and try to find out what it was that got Flipper so excited last night."

"How are you going to do that, Dad?" Sandy asked, puzzled.

"From the other side of the lagoon. The 'Shark' is a good hundred or more yards closer to that shore. With the night binoculars—"

"But, Dad!" Sandy protested. "There's nothing but trees and underbrush over there—*and* mosquitoes. And how do you figure on staying awake all night, as tired as you are? If you go, I'm going with you!"

"No, Son, you stay here—"

Sandy rarely interrupted his father, but he did so now. "I'm going with you! I'll get a sleeping bag and a Thermos of coffee. We can take turns watching. That way we can both get some sleep."

"You know something?" Porter said, grinning and clapping his son on the back. "You boys sometimes seem a lot smarter than your old man!" Then, realizing he was speaking as if Bud was there with them, the grin faded. "We'd better take along some insect repellent, Sandy."

The walk around the lagoon was not an easy one.

As with much of Coral Key Park, the land had been left in its natural state, which was to say, it was almost a jungle. The trek was made even more difficult because they did not want to use a light.

Finally they reached a point almost directly opposite the house and dock. The big schooner loomed much larger from the new vantage point, and Porter sat down at the foot of a tall coconut palm and removed the night binoculars from the carrying case. As he adjusted the focus, the deck of the "Shark" came into sharp view.

"What do you see?" Sandy whispered.

"Nothing yet. Wait. . . ." He turned the adjustment a bit more and then clearly made out the form of a man sitting atop the cabin close by the companionway hatch. "There's someone on deck." Then he saw the bright glow of a cigarette as the man took a puff. Not recalling having seen the professor smoke, he added, "I think it's Latham. Here, you have a look."

Sandy took the glasses and peered through them. "Gosh," he whispered, "it's almost as bright as day through them!"

"It won't be later on, I'm afraid. Not after the moon goes down. If anything happens, I hope it happens before then."

"Want me to keep first watch?" said Sandy.

"Okay. Wake me if you see anything at all unusual. *Anything.*"

He unrolled the sleeping bag behind the tree and stretched out on his back. He stared up through the palm fronds into the night sky for a long time, thinking. He could not bring himself to believe that Bud was dead. Still, he had no real reason for not believing it. Perhaps, he thought, it was simply a father's hope. He recalled that when the boys' mother had died, not long after Bud was born, he had felt this same disbelief. The difference then was that he knew she was dead. He did not know—not absolutely *know*—this about Bud. And as long as it could not be proved, he would hold out that thread of hope.

Porter fell into a troubled sleep, and when he woke he knew that it was much later. The stars had wheeled in the sky, and the moon had set.

"Sandy?" he whispered.

"You awake, Dad?"

"Yes. Why did you let me sleep so long?"

"I—I wasn't as tired as you, Dad, and I thought I'd let you sleep as long as you could. I was going to wake you soon. Nothing's happened. The lights have been out for a long time, but someone is still on deck. I can't tell who it is."

Porter looked at the luminous dial of his watch. "It's almost one-thirty. I wonder why they're staying up." He opened the Thermos and took a drink of hot coffee; then he asked Sandy for the binoculars. "I'll keep an eye out now. You catch some shuteye."

He peered into the binoculars. With the moon gone it was much more difficult to make out anything aboard the schooner. Something moved, however, and he saw that it was one of the men.

"I can't understand what he's staying on deck for," Porter mused.

"Latham was so mad that night Bud and I went out there, maybe he really thinks somebody might come snooping around."

"Could be. Sort of standing guard. But what would he be guarding?" Just then, as he was gazing at the dim figure of the man aboard the schooner, a slight movement at the edge of his vision caught his attention. He turned the glasses quickly in that direction. He had the briefest glimpse of a dark shape in the water, and then it blended in against the black hull of the schooner. "Hold on a minute, Sandy!" he whispered. "There's something out there!"

"What is it? Where?" Sandy stared out toward the dark outline of the "Shark," but could see nothing other than the boat.

Suddenly there was the raucous chattering of Flipper from somewhere near the schooner. The dolphin squeaked and whistled and squawked as loudly as he could.

"Dad! He's doing it again! Just like last night!" whispered Sandy. "Say, do you suppose it was Flipper that you saw?"

"I don't think so, Son. Whatever it was, I think that must be why he's setting up such a noise. Listen."

There was a heavy splash and then some more jabbering from Flipper. An angry voice drifted across the water.

"Belay that racket, you! *Belay it!*"

"That's Latham," Sandy said, grinning. "Give it to him, Flipper! Give him a squirt right in the eye!"

Just then, through the binoculars, Porter saw activity on deck. Two shadowy figures moved quickly to the rail closest to the shore. One of them seemed to lean down; then he turned and went to the companionway and vanished down the hatch. The other did the same. In a moment the first one reappeared and went back to the rail.

"Here, Sandy," Porter said. "You take a look. Maybe your eyes are better than mine. See what you make of this."

The boy took a turn at the binoculars, but he had no better luck making out what the men aboard the schooner were doing. He did notice that they appeared to be carrying something each time they went down the companionway hatch; at least, they did not move as quickly going that way as they did coming back up.

And then he noticed something else. "Dad, I could have sworn *three* people went below deck. I saw two go below, then *one* came up, and two went below again. At least, I think I saw it."

"Maybe you boys were right about hearing other voices the night you rowed out to the 'Shark.' Son, we've got to keep our eyes glued to that schooner from now until dawn. If anything moves away from it, we can't miss seeing it."

"Do you think there's some sort of boat alongside the 'Shark'?"

"There almost has to be. Against that black hull it's invisible. But if we're watching for it when it pulls away, we're bound to see it. Wait! I've got a better idea. We'll work our way back around to the dock, and when we see it pull away we can go after it in the launch."

"Now you're talking!" Sandy answered in the darkness. He lowered the glasses for a moment and looked around at his father. "Dad . . . do you think this has anything to do with what's happened to Bud?"

Porter took the binoculars and gazed through them for several moments before he answered. Then, his voice very low, he said, "Let's not get up any false hopes, Sandy."

Slowly they made their way back around the lagoon through the dense undergrowth, keeping a careful watch on the schooner as they went. By the time they reached the shore alongside the dock, the activity on board the "Shark" seemed to have stopped. If anyone remained on deck, Porter and Sandy were unable to see them. There was also no further sign of Flipper.

"If there was a boat out there," Porter said, "then it still has to be tied alongside. What I don't understand is how it got there in the first place without our hearing it."

"Maybe we've got it figured wrong," Sandy said. "We'll know when dawn comes."

They watched in silence as the minutes and hours dragged by. Shortly after four o'clock the horizon to the east began to grow light. Soon afterward the outline of the schooner began to grow clearer. A faint morning breeze stirred the surface of the calm lagoon, and the ship swung slowly on her anchor line until her bow was pointed directly at the shore where Porter Ricks and his son sat keeping their vigil. They had a clear view down both the port and starboard sides of the "Shark" and they stared in disappointment. There was only the dinghy hanging limply on its line. There was nothing else.

12. The Cave

For quite some time Bud Ricks thought that he was having a dream. He seemed to hear voices at a distance. There was a strange sort of echo sound about them, as if the people were talking inside a tunnel or a large vacant room. There was also the sound of someone or something splashing about in water. But there were none of the usual sounds of the outdoors—no birds, no sighing of the wind, no breaking of waves on the shore.

It had to be a dream. He knew that he was lying on his back, and he was very tired. He felt too tired to open his eyes, and so he simply lay there and listened.

Suddenly he became aware that one of the voices was familiar. He could even remember the last time he had heard it. It had been the night that he and Sandy rowed out to the schooner to tell Dr. Avery about the coming storm. Then, in a flash, Bud knew whose voice it was. He had only heard it a few times, but he was certain it was the voice of *Jack Finch*.

That couldn't be. Jack Finch was dead; the killer whale had gotten him. Bud stiffened. His mind was beginning to clear. His last memory came back to him. He had been in the water, and he had been starting to swim toward the skiff when he had seen *it*—the huge black fin rising slowly up from the water, and the dark shadow under the surface moving toward him. It had grabbed him and snatched him under.

"Am I inside the—the whale?" he thought. "No— no, that can't be!"

He tried to put his hand out, but something seemed to be holding it. He opened his eyes, almost afraid of what he might see. A faint light was flickering somewhere to his right. It gleamed on a damp rough surface a few feet above his face. He slowly turned his head in the direction of the light. His mind was still fuzzy, and when he saw something moving at a level slightly below him, his first thought was that it was some sort of animal. The figure straightened, and Bud saw that it was a man in a black rubber diving suit. Then he saw three other men beyond the first one. None of them was paying any attention to Bud. They were moving about, some stacking small objects on the ground, others working with diving gear. Except for a single lantern burning on a ledge near the men, there was a peculiar darkness all about.

One of the men sat down on the ledge. "Finch," he said, "try to get Mel on the radio again."

"All right. He should be tuned in now. It's about one o'clock, isn't it?"

Bud could not make out the man's face, but there was no doubt about the voice now—it was Jack Finch.

The first man looked at his watch. "One o'clock on the button."

One o'clock? Bud thought. It had been about noon when he had finished catching lobsters on the east side of Rock Island. The only explanation for all this was that he was asleep in his bed at home and was dreaming it. The bubbles in the water, the killer whale, Jack Finch—it couldn't be real!

The man was working the dials on a small radio set. He spoke into a microphone. "Bullfrog, this is Tadpole. Bullfrog, this is Tadpole. Over." Finch put a set of headphones to his ear and listened for several moments.

"This could really throw a wrench into the works," one of the men said.

"It couldn't be helped, Harry," said another. "You were out there. You saw the kid starting to nose around. The fact is, it's lucky for us he stopped instead of going in and reporting what he saw."

"You're right, Carlos," Harry replied. "And it would have been even better if Finch hadn't given the boy artificial respiration. We could have hauled his body someplace down the bay and made it look like he just fell out of the boat and drowned. No bother at all that way."

"Maybe not for you, Carlos," Finch said. "But after this job is done I've still got my conscience to live with."

"Conscience?" Carlos laughed. "Well!"

"Hold it!" Finch broke in. "I've got Mel!" In the murky darkness Finch listened intently for a moment. Then he spoke into the microphone. "Right, Bullfrog. We caught a small poacher. He's okay. We've got him in the cave. What do you suggest?"

Bud's mind churned. *The cave! Sure!* This was one of the caves under Rock Island. He had been here before. The entrance was underwater, about six feet below the surface in the reef near the north end of the island.

"What did Mel say?" Harry asked Finch.

He clicked a switch on the radio and put the microphone down. "He says to sit tight and let him keep an eye on the situation. We're to stay inside the cave until tonight."

The fourth man spoke up. "I don't like this. We could get into big trouble keeping the boy here!"

"Shut up, Pedro!" Harry snapped.

They began to argue among themselves, and Bud let his attention go to his surroundings. He still had no idea of what had happened or why he was where he was. But he did know that if he could get to the water he could hold his breath long enough to swim out through the hole and perhaps get ashore on Rock Island. The island was small, to be sure, but the undergrowth was thick, and he might be able to hide until his father came looking for him.

"First things first," he thought. "Get out of here, and then try to figure what it's all about." He rolled over on his side and tried to put his hand out. Suddenly he realized why he had not been able to move his hand before. His wrists were firmly bound together, as were his ankles. The problem now was that he had begun to roll, and he was helpless to stop himself. He was lying on a slope above the water, and he let out a yell as he gathered speed like a log going downhill. He did not stop until he reached the very edge of the water. Dazed, he felt himself being picked up and put on his feet.

"So you're conscious, eh?" said Carlos, grinning. "You see what happens to nosy kids, huh?"

"Leave him alone," Jack Finch said, shouldering his way between the others. He leaned over and untied Bud's ankles and wrists. "Are you okay, Bud?"

"I—I guess so," the bewildered boy replied. "What happened? How did I get here? I thought you—"

"Don't worry about any of that," Finch said. "Just be satisfied with the fact that you're alive. Are you hungry?"

"Yes, sir," Bud said truthfully. He looked around curiously at the other three men. They were all complete strangers, and he did not like the way they were looking at him. He was more than a little glad that Jack Finch was there.

"Get him some of those baked beans, Pedro," Finch said.

Pedro nodded and ambled off toward the lantern. He returned with the food, and Bud ate it hungrily. When the can was empty, Carlos put the ropes back on the boy's wrists and ankles.

"We have to keep you tied up, Bud," Finch said. "My advice to you is to cooperate and don't try to free yourself. You'll understand all of this after we're gone."

"Gone?" Bud said. "Are you going?"

"Not now, boy. Just don't worry yourself about it."

The four men moved away and resumed what they had been doing. Bud looked around with keen interest. He was closer to the activity than he had been before, and now in the shadows he could see that the men had been working around something in the shallow water. It appeared to be some sort of boat. Carlos and Pedro pulled it closer to the shore and began to unload something. Bud's view of it was much better now, and he suddenly realized that it was a small submarine! He had seen pictures of one similar to it. It was an open-cockpit craft, the kind that was called a "wet" submarine because the occupants were not enclosed inside it, but wore diving gear while riding in it.

Beyond the submarine, he could make out a large object that seemed to be propped against the wall of the cave. It was some distance from the lantern, and it was difficult to make it out clearly. He stared at the object for several moments, and suddenly the answer struck him with the force of a hammer!

There *was* no killer whale! This thing he was staring at was what everyone thought was a killer

whale. This tall, triangular black thing that stood propped against the wall of the cave was the fin that had been sighted at various places around the bay! Bud could make out the metal brackets with which it was fastened atop the submarine. All they had to do was cruise along just below the surface with the fake fin sticking up, and people would swear they had seen a killer whale!

Still, Bud could make no sense out of all this. What did it have to do with the "Shark" and Dr. Avery and Mel Latham? Jack Finch had been talking by radio with Latham. The talk of "Bullfrog" and "Tadpole," Bud surmised, was some sort of code. And the fact that they had a code must mean they were doing something they did not want anyone to know about.

More questions popped into Bud's mind. Why had they pretended that Jack Finch had been attacked by a killer whale? No one around Coral Key had known Finch, so why should they go to such trouble? There seemed to be only one answer to that. They must have wanted to frighten everyone off the bay so that they would have more freedom to do whatever it was they were doing.

But what *were* they doing? Bud's mind seemed to be taking him round in circles. Each answer seemed merely to bring more questions. Maybe it was some kind of spy operation! That hardly made sense; what could they be spying on from a cave beneath a small uninhabited island at the edge of a marine preserve?

Suddenly his thoughts shifted. "Oh, my gosh," he thought. "What about Dad? He's going to think the killer whale got me for sure! When they find the skiff and see that the diving mask and fins are gone, they'll know I was diving. And after what everybody thinks happened to Jack Finch, they probably won't even bother to look for me."

Bud estimated that a couple of hours had dragged past when Jack Finch busied himself at the radio again. He listened at the headphones for a time, then he said, "Roger, Bullfrog. Tadpole, out."

He put the microphone down and looked around at his companions. "Mel says everybody's out looking for the boy. The skiff has been found and people are already figuring the killer whale got the boy. We're to sit tight until after dark. He'll let us know later if he wants us to bring a load to the schooner. Mel's pretty sore about what's happened."

"Well," said Harry, "he ought to understand that it wasn't our fault. That's his part of the job, to warn

us when anybody comes nosing around out here. Why
didn't he radio that the boy was coming this way?"

"He said he saw the boy leave the lagoon, but he
was headed someplace else. He must have changed
his mind and sneaked out here. That's how kids are,
I guess," Finch said.

Harry looked over toward Bud, and after a moment he said, "What are we supposed to do with the
kid?"

A chill ran down Bud's backbone as the men all
looked in his direction.

"There were no instructions about the boy. You
know we can't do too much talking by radio. There's
not much chance of it, but somebody could be fooling
around on our frequency, and we wouldn't want anything overheard that might lead to trouble."

Pedro shook his head and sat down on the ledge.
"This thing is getting too hot for me. I say we've got
enough of the gold."

Bud's ears perked up at the mention of gold. What
gold could they be talking about? There was no gold
around Coral Key. In fact, the only mention of gold
had been in connection with that old Spanish ship,
the "El Capitan," that Dr. Avery had written about
in his book, and there was certainly no gold on it
now, Bud was sure.

"You mean you'd just go off and leave the gold that's still out there?" Carlos asked in amazement. He turned quickly toward Harry and Finch. "You see? I said Pedro would turn chicken the minute the going got rough!"

"Who's turning chicken?" Pedro demanded hotly. "I'm just saying that gold is no good to you if you're locked up in prison. I'd rather have one dollar and be free than have a hundred and be behind bars! Besides, there's plenty here in the cave and on board the 'Shark' right now. What's wrong with sailing for Cuba tonight with what we've got? Mark my words, there's going to be plenty of trouble about this kid!"

"That brings us back to the kid again," Harry said. "What do we do about him?"

"Just leave him right where he is," Pedro replied. "By the time he works loose and somebody finds him, we'll be in Havana."

"And then he spills the beans about what we've been doing? Not on your life, pal!" said Carlos. "If we pull out of here while there's still gold down there, I want to be able to come back for it when the heat's off."

There was a long silence, and Bud could feel the pounding of his heart. He *had* to get loose! They were talking about killing him!

Jack Finch spoke up finally. "You're not going to harm the boy, not while I'm around."

"We'll do whatever Mel says to do," Harry said. "And don't forget, Jack, if you ain't around, then that's one less we've got to share with."

Finch turned away. Two of the others stretched out on bedrolls and went to sleep, while Carlos busied himself with some work on the submarine. After a while, when he felt certain no one was watching him, Bud began to strain at the ropes binding his wrists. They were not so tight as to cut off the circulation of the blood, yet they were expertly tied, for no amount of twisting and pulling had the slightest effect on the knots. Finally he gave up trying. He would have to have something to cut them if he were going to get free.

Never before had he felt so completely alone. If Flipper had only come out into the bay with him, at least someone would know he wasn't dead. Flipper would have seen what happened, and he would have gone straight back and gotten his father and led him here.

But Flipper hadn't come along, and there was no way that Flipper or anyone else could possibly guess that Bud was in a cave beneath Rock Island. So, if he was to get out of this mess, he was going to have to do it all by himself. There was nothing to do now but wait and hope for some chance to get loose.

Several hours later Jack Finch had another brief conversation by radio with Mel Latham, after which the four men busied themselves with loading empty air cylinders and bars of gold onto the submarine.

"It must be night," Bud thought as Carlos and Harry got into their diving gear and got aboard the submarine. Ballast tanks fore and aft were adjusted to the load aboard the craft. A searchlight in the bow was turned on to guide them through the underwater opening, and the little vessel submerged and was gone.

Jack Finch untied Bud again, gave him some canned food and water, but would not answer any of the boy's questions. After eating, Bud lay down and fell into an exhausted sleep.

Some time later he woke to the sound of voices. He saw that the submarine was back.

"Put those refilled tanks ashore," Harry said to Pedro. He turned toward Finch. "That blasted dolphin was in the cove again! I'd like to put a bullet in him! You never heard such a racket! It's a wonder the ranger didn't come out to see what the fuss was all about."

"Don't worry about the dolphin," Finch said. "What does the situation look like?"

"About the boy? Everybody was out looking for him all afternoon and into the night. In fact, there were still some boats out when we made the run to the lagoon. When the moon set, everybody called it a night. But they'll be out again in the morning. Mel says we can count on that, and to stick here in the cave."

"I still say we ought not to push our luck," Pedro said. "We've got enough to put us all on easy street for life!"

"I told Mel about your idea, Pedro. He said to tell you we're staying here till we've got every last bit of that gold."

"Suppose somebody comes looking in this cave for the kid. What do we do then?"

"Nobody's going to come here looking for him. Why would they? Mel says the word's around that the killer whale got the kid. The search is just to make the kid's dad feel better. It won't last more than a couple of days, and then we can get back to work. Five or six more days and we should have it all."

Pedro rubbed his chin thoughtfully. "Well . . . maybe you're right."

Bud had no way of telling time. But when the submarine went out again, he figured that it must be night again. When it went out for the third time, he guessed correctly that he had been a prisoner in the cave for more than two days. Still, there had been no chance to free himself. From the conversation of his captors, he gathered that the search for him had almost entirely ceased.

He found himself longing for the sunshine that was somewhere above him. He wanted to feel the warm sea air on his cheek, and he wanted to see Flipper's happy face grinning up at him from the clear water.

"I wonder what Dad and Sandy are doing right this minute," he thought. "I—I wonder if they've given up finding me alive."

And for the first time since regaining consciousness in the cave, Bud felt the sting of tears in his eyes.

13. Rescue

Mel Latham had finished stowing the most recent cargo of gold ingots in the bilge of the "Shark," and as he came down the companionway Dr. Avery called to him from his cabin.

"Mel, I've been doing some thinking about the situation, and I've decided we should take what we have and leave immediately."

Latham leaned against the door. *"You've* decided?" he said, grinning cynically. "You ain't making the decisions, Professor. I make the decisions."

"That suited me, up until the boy became involved. In fact, you can have my share of the gold. Leave me in the cave with the boy. I'll wait twenty-four hours before I bring him out. That will give you plenty of time to reach Cuba."

"You're making me laugh, Avery. Now let me tell you something. I've decided I don't want to spend the rest of my days in Cuba. I want to be able to live right here in Florida, and that means we're getting rid of the kid. What difference does it make, anyhow? Everybody thinks he's dead."

Dr. Avery stared at the big man in amazement. "You ask what difference it makes! Simply this: Bud Ricks is as alive as you and I! *That's* the difference. And I won't let you do it, Mel. I never bargained for anything like this!"

"You bargained for your own son's life. Don't that mean anything to you now?"

The professor looked down at his clenched fists. "I don't believe my son is alive, Latham. I—I went along with this whole scheme with that in the back of my mind. You've used me—"

"You'll get your cut of the gold. Mel Latham don't back out after a deal has been made."

Dr. Avery looked up quickly into the dark face. "Then—then you admit that my son isn't alive?"

"I didn't say that. As far as I know he's in a prison camp in Cuba. I've got the connections to get him out, and I'll still go through with it if you don't mess up this operation."

"I can't do it. I can't sacrifice young Ricks. I've

got to know that the boy will not be harmed. Otherwise—"

"Otherwise what?" Latham said.

Dr. Avery straightened and looked him squarely in the eye. "Otherwise I shall go to the boy's father and tell him where his son is."

"I wouldn't try that if I was you, Professor. It wouldn't be healthy."

"Then you still intend to—to do away with the boy?"

"It's the kid's own fault. If he hadn't been nosing around out there, we could have gotten the gold and gone. Nobody would ever have been the wiser. With the kid out of the way, everything will be okay. He's got to go."

Dr. Avery turned and pulled open a drawer of his desk. When he faced around toward Mel Latham he was holding a small automatic pistol in his hand. "Then you give me no choice, Mel. Move aside. I'm going ashore and talk with Porter Ricks."

Latham stared at the gun for a moment. Then, with a faint smile, he shrugged his shoulders. "Okay, Professor. You win. If you talk to the ranger now, the whole deal will collapse. I assure you the boy won't be harmed. You've got my word on it."

"Sorry, Mel. I don't believe you. I'm going ashore."

As Dr. Avery came out of the cabin, Latham lunged at him with surprising speed. The gun clattered to the floor, and Latham's fist caught the professor solidly on the jaw. The scientist was knocked back into the cabin, and as he fell, his head struck the edge of the desk. He slumped down, unconscious.

Latham retrieved the gun and slipped it into his pocket. Then he stepped into the cabin and knelt beside the professor. "So you were going to spill the beans to the ranger, eh?" He pulled the unconscious man up and slung him over his shoulder. "I don't need you anymore, and I know just the place to put you so you don't talk to *nobody*."

He moved quickly along the passageway, through the galley, and up the companionway stairs. It was well past midnight. Stars blazed coldly overhead, and the moon hung low on the horizon. Across the lagoon the park ranger's house was dark. A single light burned on the dock.

Satisfied that no one was about, Mel Latham climbed to the deck and walked to the rail. He eased the unconscious form down toward the water and released him. "So long, Professor. Pleasant dreams!"

The body slipped beneath the surface with hardly a splash. Mel Latham stood for a moment, feet apart, gazing into the dark water. There was no sound other

than the droning of the generator and the gentle
lapping of water against the hull of the schooner.
Latham brushed at his moustache, and with a grin
of satisfaction splitting his face, he turned and disappeared down the companionway. As far as anyone would ever know, Dr. Avery had accidentally
fallen overboard during the night and drowned. If
the body was found, they would only see that he
had struck his head on something as he fell.

Moments after the big man had gone below deck,
there was a silent swirl of water a few feet from the
side of the schooner, and slowly Dr. Avery's head
emerged from the lagoon. There was a dark flow
of blood from his head wound, and his eyes were
closed. Beneath him, a powerful shape moved away
from the schooner, holding the unconscious man so
that his head remained clear of the water. It was
Flipper, and the dolphin began a slow, careful jour-
ney toward the shore. His quick mind was thinking
ahead. He could not go any faster for fear of the
water's going over the professor's face. Yet he seemed
to know that the unconscious man was going to
need the help of his fellowmen—and soon. So he
swam as fast as was safe, making unerringly for the
dock.

The single light on the dock cast an eerie glow

over the park launch and the skiff as they bobbed gently at their moorings. A faint breeze sighed in the tops of the tall palms. The unconscious body of Dr. Avery glided past the dock, and soon Flipper felt the scrape of the sandy bottom against his belly as he reached the shore. With a last surge of his powerful flukes he pushed the professor as far toward the shore as he could, leaving him lying on his back so that his face would remain out of the water. Satisfied with this, Flipper squirmed around and moved into deeper water. He poked his head up and began to squawk and whistle as loudly as he could. He flung himself up into the air and fell back with a great splash.

Almost a minute passed before he got results. The first sign was a light flashing on in Sandy's room, and then there was another in Porter's room.

"Flipper's at it again, Dad," Sandy called. "Want me to go see what it's all about?"

"We'll both go," Porter replied.

They dressed hurriedly and, with Porter in the lead, ran down toward the dock. Beyond the two boats they saw the familiar shape of Flipper as he leaped into the air, yakking and squawking loudly.

"What is it, boy?" Sandy called. "What's the matter?"

Flipper jerked his head toward the shore and swam quickly into the shallow water.

"What's that in front of him there, Son?" Porter said.

"It—it looks like there's somebody in the water!"

Together they rushed down to the water's edge and knelt beside the unconscious figure. "It's Dr. Avery! Here, Son, let's pull him up on the beach."

"The professor?" Sandy said. "How did he get here?"

"What's more important," Porter said, "is he alive?" He lifted one wrist and felt for the pulse.

"Is he. . ." Sandy began.

Porter nodded. "The pulse is strong and steady. He's alive. Now we'd better get him up to the house and call a doctor."

Just then there was the sound of a motor from the lagoon. Porter and Sandy looked out toward the "Shark." The spreader lights had been turned on, and in their glare they could see the little dinghy speeding toward shore.

"That has to be Latham," Porter said. "This is strange." He rubbed his chin thoughtfully. "How did Dr. Avery get over here?"

"I guess he swam," Sandy said.

"And then passed out when he reached shore?

Maybe. But I wonder where Flipper fits into the picture."

"Look, Dad! There's a place on the professor's head where he's bleeding! Say . . . do you suppose he might have hit his head on something and fallen overboard, and—and Flipper brought him over here?"

Porter examined the place on the professor's head. "He took quite a blow, all right." He looked out at the dolphin, who was a few yards from shore watching them. "How about it, Flipper?"

Flipper bobbed his head up and down.

"Good boy!" Porter pushed his arms beneath the unconscious scientist and lifted him gently. "You go on up, Sandy, and call Doc Young."

The dinghy came speeding alongside the dock and slid ashore on the beach. Mel Latham leaped out, barely taking time to shut off the engine.

"What happened?" he demanded of Porter. "What are you doing with the professor?"

"We found him here," Porter said. "That's all we know."

"I heard all the racket that blasted dolphin was making over here," Latham said. "Then I saw your lights and I couldn't find the professor. I guess he fell overboard."

"Go on up to the house, Sandy. Call the doctor."

"Hold on a minute," Latham said. "Lemme take a look at him." He looked at the place on the professor's head. "Don't look like much. Not much more than a bump. Just put him in the dinghy there, and I'll put something on it when I get him back aboard the 'Shark.' "

Sensing something strange in the big fellow's behavior, Porter shook his head. "We'll put him to bed up at the house. A doctor should take a look at this."

Sandy turned to make the telephone call. But Latham caught the boy's arm. "Now listen to me, both of you. Don't go sticking your noses in other people's business."

"*You* listen, mister," Porter said. "It's *my* business when anything like this happens in Coral Key Park. Now, get out of my way so I can take him up to the house! Sandy, go on and do what I told you!"

"No, you don't, sonny!" growled Latham, tightening his grip on the boy.

Just then the professor groaned and turned his head to one side. "Looks like he's coming around," Porter said. "We'll see what he wants us to do."

"What . . ." mumbled the scientist, his lips moving slowly. "Where. . . ." His eyes opened and blinked, looking first into Porter Ricks's face, then

into the scowling face of Mel Latham. "What happened?"

Porter lowered the professor to his feet. "Think you can stand up?"

"Latham!" Dr. Avery gripped Porter's arm for support, rubbing his free hand across his face and gingerly touching the wound on his head. "You. . . ."

"Come on, Professor," Latham said. He released Sandy and took hold of Avery's arm. "Let's get back to the 'Shark.' "

"Get your hands off me!" the professor snapped. He tried to pull away—weakly, for he was still dizzy and confused by what had happened to him.

"What is it, Dr. Avery?" said Porter. "Is there something we should know?"

"Yes. Yes, there is. It's your son, Bud. He's. . . ."

"He's out of his head!" Latham broke in. "He's talking crazy! Come on with me!"

Porter brusquely pushed the big man aside and spoke to the professor. "You said something about Bud. What about him?"

"The boy's alive."

Once more Latham grabbed him and pulled him roughly toward the dinghy. "He's gone off his rocker! Must have hit his head on something. Don't pay any attention to him."

Porter moved quickly between Latham and the boat. "Dr. Avery is coming up to the house, Latham. I'm going to find out what this is about Bud, and I'm going to find out right now."

"Be careful, Mr. Ricks," said the professor. "Latham is dangerous. He knows about Bud and—"

"Shut up! All of you!" Latham took a quick step back, and in the white glare of the dock light the small automatic pistol seemed to jump into his hand. "Looks like everybody's going for a little ride out to the 'Shark.' Okay, Ranger, get in the dinghy. You, too, sonny. After you, Professor."

"Bud is alive, Mr. Ricks," Dr. Avery assured Porter. "And I'm afraid you can put the blame for all that's happened on me. I've been a foolish man."

"Where's Bud? Is he aboard the schooner?"

"He's in a cave at—"

"Shut your trap, Professor!" Latham growled. "I should have made sure of you when I had the chance!" He herded his three prisoners into the dinghy and pushed it off from the beach. "You run the motor, Ranger. I'll sit here in the bow where I can keep an eye on all of you. And if you think I don't mean business with this pistol, just try something. There's nobody around here but the four of us to hear a shot."

There was no choice but to follow instructions, and Porter yanked the starter cord and eased out into the lagoon. The little boat moved across the dark water and into the light blazing down from the spreaders of the "Shark." Porter brought them alongside the schooner, and Latham motioned for them to climb aboard.

As the big fellow stood up to follow them aboard the vessel, a dark figure suddenly appeared in a flash to his right. Before Latham could so much as cry out, the sleek form came across the boat and smacked into him. The pistol clattered to the bottom of the boat, and Mel Latham, bellowing like an angry bull, went over the side into the lagoon.

"Flipper!" Sandy yelled exultantly. "Good boy, Flipper!"

Porter jumped down into the boat and picked up the gun. Meanwhile, thrashing to reach the side of the schooner, Latham found that Flipper was nosing him back with each stroke. He spluttered, cursing and shouting, trying to ward off the dolphin. He was rewarded for his efforts by loud squawks of delight from Flipper.

"We'd better get right back to shore and get the police out here," Porter said.

"You'd better call your friend at the Coast Guard,

Mr. Ricks," said the professor. "Bud is being held in one of the caves beneath Rock Island. I'll give you a complete explanation of what's happened later. The main thing now is to get the boy before he's harmed. You can use the shortwave radio here."

Latham was still trying vainly to reach the schooner. "Let him come aboard, Flipper," Porter said, laughing. "I think most of the starch is out of him now!"

The big man swam wearily to the dinghy, climbed into it, and then pulled himself onto the deck of the "Shark," dripping and sullen.

"Tie his hands behind him, Sandy—good and tight. And then, Dr. Avery, I want to hear your story."

14. An Explanation

After Mel Latham had been tied securely in a chair and Porter had contacted the Coast Guard and the police via the shortwave radio system of the "Shark," Dr. Avery began explaining. Porter Ricks poured him a second cup of steaming coffee, and the professor leaned back with a sigh.

"You see, Mr. Ricks, I have a son myself. That's how this whole fantastic scheme came about, really. My son, Ron, is twenty-six years old. He's a scientist, a botanist. He was flying to South America two years ago in a private plane, and engine trouble forced him down in Cuba. Apparently Ron had some papers in his possession that led the Communists to believe he was a spy. He was placed in a maximum-security prison outside Havana, and I've had no

official word from him since. I've tried everything—
the government, the Red Cross, everything—all to
no avail."

"Is he still alive?" Porter asked.

The professor shrugged and glanced toward Latham. "All I know for certain is that six months ago
I was introduced to this man Latham. He said he
had contacts in Cuba, that he had fought alongside
Castro in the revolution, and he might be able to
help me."

"I don't understand what that has to do with what's
happening here."

"My research for the book that Sandy has been
reading turned up quite a lot of original material. I
was in Spain working on old letters and records, and
I chanced onto a letter written by one of the surviv-
ing officers of the ill-fated 'El Capitan,' which crashed
on the reefs here. The letter explained very graph-
ically what happened, and, by comparing this with
charts of the area, I came to the conclusion that 'El
Capitan's' gold had never been salvaged, simply because it was not where the rest of the ship was."

"Somebody moved it?" asked Sandy.

"No, my boy. Do you know the reefs at the eastern
edge of the marine preserve? The ones just off Rock
Island?"

"Yes, sir, but—"

"Well, the storm first drove the 'El Capitan' across those reefs. The Spanish officer, in the letter, said very plainly that the vessel struck these reefs. The hull was ripped open and the major portion of the cargo—which included the gold—was lost at once. The fierce wind continued to drive the doomed ship across a broad bay until it finally came up against a second reef much closer to shore."

"So the gold was two or three miles from the wreck of the 'El Capitan'!" Sandy exclaimed.

"Precisely," the professor said, nodding. "I made careful calculations, and it seemed perfectly plausible to me that the gold still lay there at the first reef. One of my assistants at the university, Jack Finch, got wind of my discovery. He tried to persuade me to get the treasure, but since it was inside the restricted area of Coral Key Marine Preserve, I told him I intended to take my information to the proper authorities. Finch—"

"Jack Finch?" puzzled Sandy. "The one that the killer whale got?"

"There is no killer whale," the professor said.

"No killer whale? But—but people have seen it! There are pictures!"

"I'll explain all that in a moment. Finch, when

he found he could not convince me to get the gold illegally, then went to these men." He nodded toward Latham. "They approached me and said that in return for my son's safe return from Cuba, I would have to work with them to find the gold. They told me that if I refused, they would see to it that Ron faced a firing squad."

"Wow!" breathed Sandy.

Dr. Avery sighed. "What would any father do under those conditions? Of course I agreed to do whatever they wished. So we came here several months ago and made some exploratory dives from a small boat. My calculations were found to be correct. We located the gold and ballast stones from the 'El Capitan,' mostly encrusted with coral and almost indistinguishable from the rest of the reef unless one knew exactly what to look for. Our big problem then was to devise a way of getting it without exciting any suspicion."

Porter nodded, beginning to understand. "And so the 'Shark' was anchored here as a lookout station while divers were working at bringing up the gold."

"That's correct. There are four men out there now, all with scuba-diving equipment. We have a small submarine as well. The divers work out of the cave beneath Rock Island, and every night the submarine returns to the 'Shark' with a load of gold. They also bring in their empty air tanks and get refills."

"That's what you saw the night we watched them, Dad!" said Sandy. "And that's why we never saw it leave, because it just submerged!"

"And no doubt that was what Flipper was making so much fuss about at night," said Porter.

The professor smiled. "Indeed it was. It made Mel furious."

Porter's expression grew serious. "And these other men are holding Bud prisoner in the cave?"

The professor nodded. "Yes. The boy happened to see their bubbles while they were working on the reef. He was captured and taken to the cave. Latham was talking of—of doing away with the lad, and I simply couldn't go along with that."

"And your own boy, Ron? What about him now?" Porter said.

A look of great sadness spread over the bearded face. "I doubt very much that Ron is alive. I've thought that for some time. But you know yourself, Mr. Ricks, it's hard for a father to give up hope. Well, anyhow, I told Mel that I wasn't going through with it if Bud's life was endangered. We fought, I struck my head on something, and that's the last I remember until I came to on the shore here."

"Then Latham must have tossed you into the lagoon," Porter said, "thinking you'd drown and he would be rid of you."

"Except that Flipper brought you to shore!" Sandy said, grinning.

As if he had heard his name called, in the water near the schooner Flipper began to squawk and splash.

The sound of the park launch was heard in the distance, and in a few moments Lt. Ed Bentley and two policemen were at the side of the "Shark." The policemen immediately took charge of Latham, and Lieutenant Bentley was briefed on the situation.

"It's fantastic," he said when the professor had repeated his tale. "Do you think the men in the cave have any idea of what's happened here? I mean, is there any sort of radio contact that should be made to keep them from becoming suspicious? It seems to me we're going to need surprise on our side to make certain Bud isn't harmed."

"No, there's nothing," the professor said. "However, I do know Jack Finch, and even though the thought of gold put him in a spin, I'm certain he could no more harm the boy than I could."

Bentley shook his head. "And you say our 'killer

whale' was nothing more than an artificial fin attached to your submarine? It's amazing!"

"But it did exactly what they wanted," Porter reminded him. "It kept the bay clear while they worked."

"That it did." Bentley glanced at his wristwatch. "I sent the picket boat around with half a dozen of my men in diving equipment. They should be getting here any minute now."

"There are one or two other things, Dr. Avery," Porter said. "That fin that Bud found on the beach —whose was it?"

"It apparently was lost by one of the men on the submarine. It was a bit embarrassing until someone suggested the tide could have brought it there."

"And the picture that was taken of the 'killer whale' far down the bay? What was your submarine doing there?"

"Simply putting in an appearance to keep people aware of the killer whale's presence."

There was the sound of powerful engines near the schooner, and the Coast Guard picket boat came alongside.

Flipper preceded the rescue party into the cave at Rock Island by a brief moment. Bud and Jack

Finch were the only ones awake when Flipper surfaced in the underground pool and blew. The other three—Carlos, Pedro, and Harry—were sound asleep on their bedrolls.

They woke immediately when Flipper poked his head up, saw Bud, and began to jabber with delight. Carlos made a dash for a gun lying on the ledge, but when divers began to pop up all over the pool, he meekly laid it aside and put his hands into the air.

It was almost dawn when the entire group arrived back at Coral Key in the picket boat. Jack Finch and Dr. Avery were allowed to remain, while the others were taken off to keep Mel Latham company.

As soon as Bud had gotten something to eat, he asked Porter, "Dad, what will they do to Mr. Finch and Dr. Avery?"

"I think the circumstances will speak for themselves, Son. They did what was right in the end. Neither of them was going to agree to your being harmed."

"Gee, that's swell!" the boy said, obviously relieved. Suddenly his eyebrows shot up. "Dad! Now that there's no killer whale, it's okay to go in the water, isn't it?"

"Sure, Son. Anytime you want to."

"*Yippee!*" Bud yelled, and he streaked down to

the dock, where he dived into the water without a pause. Flipper was waiting, and Bud grabbed hold of the dolphin's dorsal fin. Flipper squawked with pleasure and went darting across the lagoon in the early morning light with his young passenger.

"Boys will be boys, eh?" laughed the professor.

"And thank heaven for that," Porter said.